Mr Mac

Lesley

Best wishes —

Margaret Rice

Mr Mac

The final book of a trilogy of stories

by

Margaret Rice

Illustrated by
Marlene Keeble

TDF

ISBN 978-0-9569998-2-5

Printed and bound in the UK by
CPI Antony Rowe, Chippenham

First published in the UK in 2013 by

TDF Publishing
Sleaford, Lincolnshire

For all those Irish feral cats
who entered and enriched my life
with their unfailing affection
and devotion

and
for all those with loving hearts
still out there, who have not yet
been given the chance to do the
same for others of my kind;

also for a certain little
marmalade gentleman
with impeccable manners

Published 2011

Published 2012

With sincere thanks to
my old friend and trusted literary critic,
Pauline Seeley;

also to Jan & Haydn Wesley, without whose
encouragement it is doubtful any of this
trilogy of tales ever would have been told;

and, finally, my everlasting love and gratitude
go to all the animals whose lives and
personalities were the inspiration for the stories
in which they appear, as themselves.

In memory of a very dear young friend

Digger

A loving and gentle soul, so sadly missed

Contents

The Challenge

A small figure, just a dot in the landscape, stood up from his resting place and looked about him.

There was not another living creature anywhere to be seen in the vastness of the countryside around him.

He was alone.

He was tired, hungry and thirsty, and very anxious. He had no idea where he was, to where he was headed, or what would become of him.

He was a novice at the craft of surviving in the wild, but he knew enough to know he couldn't stay there, where he had rested, out in the open, without shelter, food or water.

He had to keep going.

With a heavy heart, and a weary body, he walked on.

Welcome To The World

Mac's earliest memories of life were when his eyes began to open at ten days old, and he saw his parents for the first time.

Smiling down on him was his mother. He saw that she was a dainty brown and black tabby cat, with the most beautiful smile.

Standing behind her, was his father. He too was smiling at him.

He saw that his father was identical in colour to his mother, and then, looking down at his own legs and paws, he saw he too was the same colour.

Mac didn't know it, but all three of them were true to the colour and stature of their wild cat ancestors. Their bodies were compact, borne on sturdy, shortish legs, and they had rather large heads, but with short ears, rounded at the tips. Their perfect camouflage colouring of brown and black striped and speckled tabby coats were complemented by the all black pads of their paws. While Mac had a smudge of white around his mouth, there was not one hair of any colour other than brown and black anywhere on the bodies of his parents.

Mac's mother spoke first.

"Well dear," she said softly, "what do you think of us?"

Mac smiled and said, "I love you Mamma, and you too, Papa."

His father spoke, "My beautiful boy, we love you too, so very, very much."

Mac's parents had been disappointed when Mac was born, having been blessed with just the one kitten, when they had been expecting more, but that disappointment was immediately dispelled by their delight that their only son was of average size and quite obviously very healthy. The fact that he favoured them both so very closely for coat colour was an added bonus.

Although Mac had had no clear recollection of suckling his mother's warm sweet milk in the days before his eyes had opened, now, suddenly, he was very hungry.

He turned to his mother and smiled.

She understood, saying to his father, "I think any further introductions will have to wait, he's hungry again."

His father nodded, and retreated to sit up on a bale of hay, while Mac's mother tended to their kitten's needs.

When Mac had drunk his fill, he burped loudly, and, with a wind inspired lop-sided smile,he said to his mother, "I feel sleepy now, I just …..", he yawned widely, "I just ….. I just can't seem to stay awake."

His mother cuddled him to her, and, under the watchful eye of his father, and the comforting rasp of his mother's rough tongue on the back of his neck, in no time at all Mac was fast asleep.

His parents smiled at one another as they watched Mac sleeping peacefully. They were so very proud of their beloved only son.

Finding Friends

As Mac began to grow, like all kittens of his age, he was very active, and very keen to explore his surroundings.

He explored every inch of the old barn in which he had been born, and quickly knew by name each of the cattle, and the donkey, who shared his home.

There was Daisy, a very pretty chestnut and white cow, who spent most of each day caring for her young daughter, Primrose. Then there was Daisy's sister, Bluebell, who was the same colour as her sister, but was still awaiting the birth of her calf.

Always in the company of the two cows, was Murphy.

He was a very elderly donkey, who had had a long working life during the days when donkey power had been valued for farm work, and who, in recognition of his long days of selfless toil, had been granted a quiet and comfortable retirement.

He, Daisy, and Bluebell were close friends, and Murphy saw his job now as being there to watch over the cows and their offspring, to keep them all safe from harm.

At his advanced age, Murphy was a stickler for old fashioned etiquette and, while he expected the youngsters to address him as "Mr." Murphy, he also afforded them the same courtesy by addressing them as "Miss" Primrose and "Mr." Mac.

It was Spring, and the cattle and donkey were now spending more and more of their time outdoors, to enjoy the sunshine while they grazed contentedly on the pastureland which adjoined the barn.

Mac and young Primrose had become close friends, and expended the boundless energy of their youth, playing together in the field, mostly chasing one another in endless games of tag.

With Primrose's cousin not yet arrived, and with Mac having no siblings for playmates, Primrose's mother and Mac's parents were grateful for the youngsters' friendship, which had the undeniable advantage of relieving them of the responsibility of the unenviable task of trying to keep two lonely youngsters amused, and they looked on contentedly as kitten and calf dashed hither and thither together.

Mac had had some sense of concern that once his friend Primrose had her cousin for a playmate, she might not want him, but the arrival of Jasmine (or "Miss" Jasmine as she was to Murphy) was to put his mind at rest on that score.

Just as soon as her legs were steady enough to support her weight, Jasmine enthusiastically joined the play team, and, like Primrose, she didn't seem to notice that Mac was not a calf.

Murphy had had some reservations about the strange combination of kitten and calves playing together, but even he quickly became convinced that there was no harm in it and no cause for concern.

Mac had other friends too. He was so amiable by nature, he quickly gained the confidence and won the friendship of a squirrel who lived in the woodland beyond the field.

He and Sidney played together, and Sidney showed him the ways of the wild wood, schooling him in the valuable lesson of the art of climbing using the least amount of energy, and, the less valuable lesson for a cat, of how to decide, later in the year, which nuts were ready for harvesting and storing for the Winter.

Mac made friends too with a young deer named Deirdre, and a pheasant called Phyllis, to both of whom the woodland was also home.

While Deirdre was happy to play tag with Mac, Phyllis was advancing in years, and most certainly did not want to run around, wasting valuable energy.

To Mac's surprise, Deirdre proved to have a greater degree of alacrity and turn of speed than either of his young calf friends, and, as Mac tried, unsuccessfully, to catch her as she dodged in and out of the trees, Phyllis would sit on the field wall watching them, and 'tutting' her disapproval of such energy wasting hi-jinks.

Phyllis liked Mac though, and very much appreciated his company at those times when, despairing of ever catching Deirdre as she peeped out from behind one tree and then, seconds later, from behind another, he would give up and return to sit beside her on the wall.

There, she would regale him with tales of her long life, all the chicks she had raised, and of how, for years, she had managed to outwit the humans with guns who had tried to shoot her.

Then, she would look sad, and, more to herself than to Mac, she would speak softly of lost family members and friends who had not been as lucky as she.

Mac had been shocked at the indifference and callousness with which her loved ones had been taken from her.

He learned much about human behaviour from Phyllis.

Growing Up

Life for Mac continued in an energetic and happy daily round of play and learning, and it was not until he had grown considerably that his parents had a serious talk with him about his future independence.

It was then that, in common with other growing kittens of his age, he understood, and accepted, that one day he would leave his parents, to go to a new home of his own.

He was excited at the prospect of adventure in new, and as yet, unexplored surroundings, but was sorry too to think that, when that time came, he would have to leave the pals of his kittenhood behind.

Already though, Primrose and Jasmine were growing up and were noticeably less inclined to play and, anyway, they were now so tall that as they stood, towering above him, Mac had to shout to them to make himself heard.

The same was true of Deirdre and, with Sidney having less and less time available to play, as he became more and more preoccupied with planning for the nut gathering season to come, the only one of his kittenhood friends who remained truly unchanged was Phyllis, who, as ever, continued to grumble about 'crazy youngsters' who had no sense of responsibility about conserving energy for use when it was actually needed.

Almost before he knew it, there loomed the day for his

departure into a life independent of his parents.

During the day before Mac left for his new home in Co.Cork, he was careful to make sure that he saw each of his friends of his kittenhood, to say goodbye to them, to thank them for all the good times they had had together, and to tell them that he would never forget them.

It was now late Summer, and with Daisy, Bluebell, Primrose and Jasmine spending their days and nights outdoors, finding them in the field was no problem. Mac located Sidney too without difficulty, but then found himself forced to spend almost the entire day seeking out Deirdre.

When, eventually, he did track her down, she was delighted to see him, and was flattered that he had gone to so much trouble to find her.

By then it was getting late in the day, and, as he had strict instructions from his parents to be home punctually, for them all to spend their last evening together, he and Deirdre had time only for a brief exchange of goodbyes, and to wish each other good luck for the future, before Mac had to hurry away.

Mac still had Phyllis to see, and so, with no time left now to go searching for her as well, as he emerged from the woodland, it was with considerable relief that he saw his friend sitting quietly on the field wall.

To his surprise, old Phyllis became quite emotional, telling him of how much she had enjoyed his company and of how very much she would miss him.

She beseeched him to take good care of himself, to be

wary around humans as not all of them could be trusted, and to think of her once in a while. She also told him that if ever he found himself in trouble, as her friend, he could rely on any pheasant to help him, and, in that situation, he must tell the pheasant that Phyllis could vouch for him.

As they said goodbye to one another, Phyllis fluffed out her feathers, settled down closer on to the wall and then her voice faltered as she said to him, "Now, I need to rest, so be off with you ….." she peered at him intently, "and remember, don't waste energy doing foolish things."

Then she closed her eyes, and Mac knew she expected him to go.

What he didn't know was that just as soon as he had turned and started off for home, old Phyllis' eyes flew open again and, with a heavy heart, and her tears blurring her vision, she watched her young friend walking away from her, and out of her life.

With his amiable disposition, Mac had brought sunshine into the twilight years of old Phyllis' life. He had touched her heart,and she was going to miss him.

As he had promised to do, Mac arrived home punctually, and was greeted at the door of the barn by his parents, who had been anxiously awaiting his return.

After tea, Mac and his parents sat together, and talked late into the evening.

His parents told him of how much they loved him and that when he left the next day, their love would go with him. He would always be in their thoughts, and, wherever he went, and whatever he did, he must remember that their love for him would always be with him.

Mac told his parents that his love would always be with them too.

They reminded him to remember to be respectful to others, and not to allow others to be disrespectful to him.

Irrespective, however, of how others around him might conduct themselves, they expected him to be polite and well mannered at all times.

They told him he was intelligent, and his exceptionally amiable disposition would stand him in good stead. He made friends easily (at this point, his parents smiled to themselves as they thought of his motley collection of friends), and that would be of great benefit to him for the future, as he would never be lonely for company.

He must remember too that there were special rules to be followed when invited into the interior of a human's home: He must explore only to the extent to which he had been specifically invited to do so. However tempting, there must be no sharpening of claws on any of the furniture or furnishings, and, under no circumstances whatsoever, was fouling indoors permitted.

His parents thought about that last one for a moment, before his father corrected it with, "But we know some humans do give cats a tray of litter for the purpose, and so, if you are absolutely sure that is what it is, and it is intended for you, then it will be all right for you to use it."

There seemed to be so much to remember that Mac was beginning to feel confused, and was becoming a bit anxious about not forgetting any of it. He was wondering if he would actually be able to cope when he was on his own.

His parents noticed his anxiety, and smiled at him reassuringly, telling him that they were sorry and that they had not intended to alarm him with their advice. They stressed that there was absolutely nothing for him to worry about. They were general guidelines only. He was a bright boy, and it would take him no time at all to decide on what was appropriate behaviour in his new home.

Mac hoped they were right, and, when he went off to bed that night, he lay awake for some time.

He was excited at the prospect of his big day tomorrow, but, despite his parents' assurances, he was still a little apprehensive about what his new family and his new home would be like.

He loved his parents so much, he was so very anxious not to let them down.

Orla

As little Orla and her parents stepped out of their car, the three cats were watching, and Mac and his parents liked what they saw.

Orla was a pretty little six year old, with bright cornflower blue eyes and curly blonde hair.

Orla's mother was an older version of her daughter, with blue eyes, curly blonde hair, and a serene, kind and gentle expression.

The child's father was tall, with twinkling blue eyes, and light brown hair. He too had a kind face, and the cats could see that he was smiling cheerily.

All three were the sort of humans who were liked, and could be trusted, by members of the animal kingdom.

Orla smiled up at her parents as her mother took her hand and all three headed across the yard towards the cats.

The child stooped and offered her hand to Mac, saying, "Hello, Mac, I'm Orla, and I would like to be your friend, if you will let me."

She smiled prettily at him and started to stroke him.

Still stroking him gently, she reassured Mac's parents with, "I promise I will look after him, and I just know we're going to have a great time together."

Then she sat down on the step into the barn, and invited Mac on to her lap.

He obliged, and purred loudly and happily as Orla continued to talk to him softly, and to stroke him.

Her parents looked on, smiling.

Her mother said to her father, "Well, that seems to be a great success."

"Yes," said her father, "certainly she likes him, and he seems to be very happy with her."

Indeed Mac *was* very happy. He hadn't known quite what to expect and had been a bit anxious, but now he knew he couldn't have asked for better than Orla. She was going to be a wonderful friend to him.

"Well, Orla," said her mother, "let's give Mac time now to say goodbye to his parents." Although Orla was reluctant to be parted from her brand new friend, she said, "Yes." and obediently followed her parents back across the yard, to stand by the car, while they waited for Mac to join them, when he was ready to do so.

First Mac's mother hugged him tightly to her, saying tearfully, "Now, be a good boy and be happy ..... we ..... we will miss you," she paused, and her voice trembled as she went on, "but, but you're going to have such a wonderful life now with Orla, and we're so happy for you."

Then Mac's father hugged him and told him how proud they were of him, on this, his big day.

Mac thanked his parents for all they had done for him, and he told them how much he loved them, and always would love them.

Then, they stood back and, with tears in their eyes, they let him go. Mac trotted over to join Orla and her parents.

Orla stroked him again, and he turned and waved

goodbye to his parents before the little girl lifted him gently and placed him into a comfortable travelling basket, ready for the journey to the family's home in Co.Cork.

Then they were all in the car, and were leaving.

Mac's parents continued to stare after them, waving goodbye to their beloved only son, until the car carrying him away from them was out of sight. It was not until then that they turned, and walked back slowly into the barn.

Mac's mother still had tears in her eyes.

His father squeezed her paw, and said softly, "He'll be just fine."

His mother dabbed away her tears, and said, "Yes, yes I know he will. She's such a lovely little girl. Mac is very lucky."

"Yes," said Mac's father with a wry smile, "and so is the little girl."

They smiled at each other. They would miss Mac enormously, but were so very proud of him.

Away Into A New Life

It was a lengthy journey to Cork, and, being Mac's first experience of car travel, at first he was a little nervous of the sounds and movements of the vehicle.

He and Orla were side by side on the back seat of the car, and the little girl placed her hand on his basket, and talked to him softly for the entire journey. The sound of her voice reassured him, and, squinting through the lid of the basket, he could glimpse her smiling face.

It did not take long for him to relax in what he knew to be the safety of Orla's company and care – so much so that, during the second half of the journey, he drifted off to sleep, and, much to the amusement of Orla's parents, was snoring loudly!

On his arrival at his new home, Mac discovered that Orla and her parents lived in a modest, but very pretty old house, located towards the top of a hill, beside a quiet country lane.

To one side of the house was an expanse of raised lawn, set above an old stone retaining wall beside the drive into the property. There were trees at each end of the boundary wall beside the lawn, and, over the wall, farmland extended away into the distance.

From the vantage point of the lawn, there was a panoramic view over the surrounding countryside, and in one direction, and on a clear day, a tiny sliver of blue on the horizon could be seen, which Orla would later tell Mac was the sea.

Immediately to the front of the house were shrubs and a small lawn, and, beyond the wall on that boundary, was pastureland, where cattle grazed peacefully in the sunshine.

The old house occupied an island of prettily cultivated gardens in a sparsely populated, tranquil rural setting.

It was safe, and absolutely perfect for children and cats.

Best Friends

Mac liked his new home ..... and he adored Orla.

He and the child were inseparable.

He had a bed and everything else he needed in a small room next to the kitchen, but, early on, Orla had pleaded with her parents for him to be permitted to sleep on her bed with her at night, and so quickly his own bed had become little used.

His room also housed the family's washing machine – something he had not seen before – but Orla had sat with him on her lap the first time it was switched on, to reassure him that the noise it made wouldn't hurt him.

Once he had become accustomed to its noise, he and Orla spent many happy times together, while he looked in through the glass of the porthole window, watching in fascination at the whirling around and around of the laundry. She smiled and laughed as she watched him following the swirling laundry with his eyes.

The days when Orla was at school passed slowly for Mac, and for her.

On school days, he would spend some time keeping her mother company, but most of the time he spent asleep. If the weather was fine, he would sleep in the garden in the sunshine, but, if not, he would be snuggled up cosily in his own bed, while he awaited his friend's return.

Whatever the weather, always he was waiting at the front gates when Orla was due home. He came to recognize the sound of the school bus approaching and would pace up and down while he waited for it to come into sight, and stop outside the gates.

The first thing Orla would do as she came in through the gates was to fling down her school bag and pick him up, to cuddle him, to the accompaniment of his loud purrs of welcome.

The weekends were bliss for Mac, as he and Orla could spend almost all of their time together, the child being very reluctant to leave him, even when tempted by her parents with what promised to be very enjoyable outings for her.

Orla and Mac were blissfully happy together, and Orla's parents were delighted with their choice of companion for their cherished only child.

Storm Clouds On The Horizon

Mac had lived with Orla and her parents for more than a year when he first began to notice changes in his friend.

Although just as affectionate towards him, Orla was pale and lacked her usual enthusiasm, energy, and sense of fun.

In the past when she had returned home from school, she had played energetically with Mac, to the extent that it was always with great reluctance that she obeyed her mother and went indoors for her tea.

Now, after greeting Mac and cuddling him, she was too tired for more than a few minutes of play with him, opting instead for picking him up and taking him indoors, to sit beside her while she waited for her tea to be ready.

She went to bed early, but, in the morning, after a full night's sleep, she was still pale and tired.

Mac knew Orla's parents were worried about her. From their conversations he overheard, he knew his friend had been taken to doctors and hospitals for tests.

He missed her desperately each time she had to stay in hospital for treatment.

As the weeks wore on, Orla became weaker and weaker, and more and more tired.

Some days she went to school, but more often she did not, and would spend the day in bed.

Again, it was from an overheard conversation between

Orla's parents that Mac learned Orla was very sick indeed. All the treatments she had undergone had failed, and nothing more could be done for her. Mac's friend was going to die.

From then on, Mac didn't want to leave her side, and, on the days she spent in bed, she would lie there awake, stroking and talking to him. He felt her fear.

A Time Of Sorrow

It was towards the end of the Summer, when Orla was spending most of every day in bed, that Mac sat with her constantly, often missing his own meals because he would not leave her side.

On sunny afternoons, he would watch the shafts of sunlight coming in through her bedroom window, to dance on the pale face of his friend, with a warm breeze softly sighing into the room, gently billowing and fluttering the net curtains at the sides of the open window.

On that last day, the one he would never forget, Orla was asleep. Mac snuggled up close to her and rested his head against her arm. She smiled in her sleep, and murmured, "Mac".

He stayed on her bed with her throughout the whole of the day.

For some time now, Orla's parents had taken turns to sit at their daughter's bedside throughout each night, and it was not until when, late into the night, her father had risen from the chair to exchange places with his wife, and had left to get some sleep, that Mac fell into the deep sleep brought on by anxiety and exhaustion.

Very early the next morning, Mac was awoken not by birdsong, but by the weeping of Orla's mother, who was holding her little daughter's hand in hers, and sobbing as if her heart would break.

During the night, little Orla's earthly life had ended peacefully for her in her sleep. Cancer had claimed another young life. Orla was still just seven years old.

Knowing that Orla had not had long to live, Mac was not surprised by her death, but he was shocked at the realization that his beloved little friend was now gone from him, for ever.

Never again would they sit together under the trees while she read to him from her books, never again would they share their toys and play together, never again would he hear her sweet voice, or feel her gentle touch as she stroked his head, and never again would he meet her at the gates when she came home from school.

His heart ached with sorrow for the loss of his best friend.

He stayed on Orla's bed, tears rolling down his cheeks, as, silently, he told her, over and over again, of how much he cared for her, and of how much he would miss her, until, at Orla's mother's request, her father came into the room and lifted Mac gently from his little daughter's bed.

"C'mon now, Mac, it's time for you to have your breakfast .....", his voice faltered, "Orla wouldn't have wanted you to miss that, now would she?"

Mac's breakfast was ready for him in his room, and, after telling him gently that he could see her again later, Orla's father closed the door on him.

Mac was too distressed to eat, and spent the remainder of the day miserably in his bed, thinking of, and weeping for, Orla.

Late that evening, Orla's father kept his promise to Mac and collected him from his room, to go to see Orla.

Mac was allowed to stay for a while on her bed, where he kept silent vigil beside his friend.

Orla's parents sat side by side at her bedside, and it distressed Mac greatly to see them so stricken with grief. Their pale, drawn faces gave them the appearance of lifeless alabaster statues as they sat, without speaking, in the darkened room.

Mac longed to give them comfort, but didn't know what he could do because they were so locked into their own grief for their little daughter, he could see that their expressionless eyes didn't even notice him.

Eventually, Orla's father rose, and, just before he picked him up again, Mac was able to gently touch Orla's hand, and to whisper goodnight to her.

Then, he was being carried from Orla's bedroom and returned to his own room for the night.

In the closed world of grief she now inhabited, Orla's mother didn't even notice he was gone.

The next Mac saw of Orla was on the day of her repose at the house.

Unnoticed, he had sneaked into her bedroom, and the beauty of the scene which met his eyes made him weep.

Orla's little white framed bed was decked with flowers. She lay beneath a white lace bedspread strewn with the blooms of fresh flowers. Her hands were rested on the bedspread, and were clasped around a small posy of flowers. On her head was a circlet of flowers resting on her beautiful golden curls.

Although pale and still, he had never seen his friend look more beautiful, and, at that moment, he believed he had glimpsed an angel.

He stayed in the room, quietly gazing at this vision of beauty which was his friend, until he heard the sounds of cars and voices outside.

Then he heard the outer doors of the house being opened, and, a minute or two later, Orla's parents came into the bedroom.

Orla's mother sat to one side of the bed, with her husband standing beside her, and, as the first of those who had come to pay their respects entered the room, Mac retreated, unseen, and returned to his own room.

In the weeks that followed, Mac missed Orla desperately, and never before had he been so unhappy.

All his attempts to comfort Orla's parents had failed miserably. Her mother avoided him, and, although her father did continue to interact with him, all the while he was distracted and seemed scarcely aware that Mac was there as he absent mindedly stroked him.

The house was such a quiet and lonely place for Mac without Orla.

He had no company all day long. Whereas before, he and Orla's mother had kept each other company while they waited for Orla to come home from school, now her mother had taken to going out every day.

She fed Mac and kept his room clean and tidy, but once

Orla's father had left to go to work, she would leave to go somewhere, anywhere, to get away from her now silent and empty home, and the cat who reminded her so painfully of her little lost daughter.

And so it was that Mac spent every weekday on his own. He was lonely for company, and very unhappy as he struggled with his own grief for his friend.

It was about a month after Orla's death that Mac overheard a conversation between her parents and realized it was about him.

Orla's mother was speaking, "I'm sorry," she said, "but Orla loved him so much ….. they were always together and now ….. and now, I can't bear to see him without her."

She burst into tears, and it was a while before she could go on, "I know it's unfair to him and it's making him unhappy ….. and ….. and Orla wouldn't have wanted that, but I can't help how I feel."

"Yes, I know," said her husband sympathetically, "I do understand."

His wife went on, "We're making him unhappy, and he's making us unhappy, and I just don't know what to do about it."

"I know, I know," Orla's father said anxiously, "but we'll have to think of something."

Overhearing their conversation made Mac feel even worse, knowing now, for sure, that not only had he failed to comfort his friend's parents, he was actually making them even more unhappy.

He went to his room, climbed into his bed, and, covering

his eyes with his paws, he wept in utter despair.

Mac lay awake in his bed late into the night. It was a household of sorrow, and, as things stood, he could think of no solution to return it to the happy house he had known with Orla.

It was about two weeks after that conversation between Orla's parents that Mac heard them discussing him again.

Orla's father was telling his wife that he had run into an acquaintance. He had told him about Orla dying, and about Mac, and immediately the man had offered to have Mac. He was a kindly man he had known for a number of years, and, even better, there were two children of around Orla's age in the family, and so Mac would have someone to play with him again.

Mac heard Orla's mother ask, "They will be good to him, won't they?"

"Yes," he replied, "I'm sure he will be just fine there."

"Well, if you're sure ….." Orla's mother didn't finish her sentence.

"Yes," he said, "and it's the chance for Mac ….." he stopped and corrected himself, "….. it's the chance for all of us to move on and to begin to re-build our lives."

"What would Orla think?" asked his wife.

"Look," said her husband, gently, "we're unhappy, he's unhappy, and Orla would never have wanted that for any of us."

Orla's mother fell silent. On the one hand it was a solution to an unhappy situation, but on the other there was an uncomfortable feeling of guilt about sending Mac away to another home.

That feeling did not go away, and, after Mac had left for his new home, Orla's mother was to silently ask for her little lost daughter's forgiveness for parting with her friend.

Another Home

Orla's parents had tears in their eyes as they said goodbye to him and told him they were sorry, but making each other unhappy could not go on.

Mac understood why they were sending him away, but he didn't want to go, and he sat, miserably slumped in a heap in a corner of his travelling basket, all the way to Kerry.

"What's the matter with it?" demanded the girl child, as she gazed down on Mac, who had remained huddled up in a corner of his travelling basket after the basket had been opened.

"Give him a chance," said her father, "he doesn't know us and he needs us to give him time to settle in."

"But I want to play with him now." cried the girl, sulkily pouting her lip.

"Well, I'm sorry, but you'll have to wait until tomorrow." said her father.

The girl didn't reply. Instead, turning back to Mac, she poked him hard in the ribs with her finger.

"Ouch." yelped Mac.

"Oh, that's livened him up a bit." said her brother gleefully, and then, before his father had the chance to stop him either, he too poked Mac in the ribs, and made him yelp again.

The children's father intervened.

"Stop that." he said sternly, "Leave him alone."

Mac was grateful to him. He was tired from the journey, and unhappy, and all he wanted now was to be shown to his bed, where he could curl up and let sleep take away his cares for a few hours.

The children's mother spoke up, saying to her husband, "Don't say that to them, he's their cat, and it's only right they want to play with him."

"Not like that," her husband retorted sharply, "we have to consider his welfare too."

The children's mother bridled with resentment. She was not accustomed to her husband contradicting her opinion, and she didn't like it one little bit. As the annoying difference of opinion with her husband had been over Mac, she blamed him for the incident, and so rested her resentment upon him. There and then, she vowed to herself that no cat was going to be allowed to cause trouble in *her* home.

Unfortunately for Mac, through no fault of his own, already he had made an enemy of one of the two people upon whom he now relied for his livelihood.

Unaware of his wife's resentment, the children's father picked up Mac, and, despite his children's protestations, carried him away to his bed.

There, Mac purred his thanks as the man stroked him, and then left him.

Mac settled down into his bed, and then quickly drifted off into sleep, to spend the next few hours very happily in the company of his beloved friend, Orla, who joined him in the land of dreams.

Resolutions

When he awoke the next morning, Mac felt refreshed, and more positive.

He reasoned that although he didn't like the look of these children at all, he was there, in their home, he had no choice, and so he would have to make the best of it.

Sadly for Mac, his positive approach to his new home was not to bear fruit.

Unlike Orla, these two children to whom he was now entrusted were not kind, or gentle. They didn't want a devoted companion. What they wanted, and expected, was a submissive animal whom they could tease, dominate, and make demands upon for their own entertainment. Their idea of playing with Mac was to force him into trying to perform silly, demeaning tricks.

Nevertheless, Mac did his best to please them, but, they lacking the patience to allow him the time to understand what it was they wanted him to do, when, inevitably, he got it wrong, the children shouted at him, told him he was stupid, and slapped him.

Never before in his life had he been slapped, and, the first time it happened, with his rump stinging from the blow, he just stood there, staring at the children in disbelief, whereupon they laughed at him, and hit him again.

After that first time, whenever either of the children slapped him, he ran away and hid.

It was fortunate for Mac that it did not take long for the children to became frustrated by their lack of success to get him to perform tricks, and for them to decide he was too stupid to learn anything. It was then that they lost interest in him and, from then on, ignored him.

With the children totally disinterested in his welfare, and their father, Mac's only ally in that household, away from home for several days of each week, it fell to the children's mother to feed Mac.

As her two very spoilt, selfish children were now totally disinterested in him, and, from that first day, she had resented his presence in her home, sometimes she fed him, but at other times either forgot, or didn't bother.

With the children's father's job continuing to keep him away from home for much of the time, it was only on those days, when he was home, that life was bearable for Mac.

Blissfully unaware of what went on in his absence, the children's father had no idea of the neglect and indifference Mac was suffering at the hands of his family when he was not around.

Although Mac had made up his mind to make the best of the new life which had been thrust upon him, as time went on, he found himself spending more and more of each day in the garden, hiding away out of sight.

There he sat, for hours on end, lonely and unhappy, weeping and thinking of his beloved Orla and wishing her back with him.

Often at the height of his misery and despair, he would think too of Phyllis. Was weeping and longing for someone who couldn't return to him a waste of valuable energy? He didn't know, but what he did know was that he couldn't help himself. He was so unhappy that remembering his dearest friend was his only comfort in his abject despair.

And so it was that the long, lonely days and nights passed slowly by for poor Mac.

More Changes

Mac had been with the family for about six months when the first of many weekends away began.

The children's father's job took him far and wide all over the country (which is how Orla's father made his acquaintance in the first place) and now, whenever a Friday found him in a particularly suitable place for his wife and children to enjoy, they would set out that day, to join him for the weekend.

The children's father thought about Mac's welfare, but accepted, without question, his wife's assurances that she had made arrangements for him to be fed and cared for in their absence.

In reality, she had done no such thing, and, instead, had shut Mac out of the house, to fend for himself until they returned.

Never having had any experience of gleaning a living from the countryside, Mac remained with nothing to eat or drink for the time the family was away.

Still blissfully unaware of what was actually going on, when the children's father was at home, it was unfortunate for Mac that still he didn't notice anything amiss.

Towards the end of Mac's time with the family, the children's father was sent overseas by his employer for several weeks, and there was then the chance for his wife and children to join him for a holiday during the last two weeks of his business trip.

Once again, the children's mother assured her husband that Mac was in good hands in their absence, whereas, in reality, while locking the door of their home as she and the children were about to leave, to go to the airport, she had ignored Mac, and had made no attempt whatsoever to stop her children chasing him away from the house.

For the first two days of their absence, as he had during the family's weekends away, Mac went without anything to eat or drink.

At the end of the third day, however, when, to his dismay, there was still no sign of their return, he knew he would have to find something to eat and drink for himself.

When he awoke at first light the next day, he considered what to do. He had been locked out of the house, and he knew there was nothing to eat, or to slake his thirst, in the garden.

Later that morning, he set off into the surrounding countryside, in search of both.

In the open countryside, he could find nothing to eat, but, some distance away from his home, he discovered a small stream of cool water running down the hillside.

He lapped the water gratefully, and, until he had begun to drink, he had not fully realized just how thirsty he had become.

He was just wondering where to go next in search of food, when he spotted a cottage, nestled into the hillside, about a hundred metres downstream from where he had been drinking.

He trotted off at a brisk pace.

As he approached the cottage, all appeared deserted.

He pushed his way through the bushes surrounding the front garden, and walked up to the front of the cottage.

There was no-one about, and so he ventured cautiously around the house, into the garden at the rear of the property.

Then he saw it.

In the centre of the garden there stood a pole, on the top of which was a platform, and that platform was laden with food scraps.

He stood at the bottom of the pole, looked up, and sniffed the air.

The food had an appetising smell to it, and his tummy rumbled at the prospect of eating, at last.

The problem remained though of how to reach the platform.

The pole was slim and smooth, offering very little grip for climbing. It would have defeated most cats, but, fortunately for Mac, he had had the advantage of Sidney's tuition, and so, remembering all Sidney had taught him of climbing techniques to suit all occasions, after a few abortive attempts, he was hauling himself up on to the platform and was about to tuck into the feast laid out before him.

He ate all that was there.

During the remainder of the two weeks the family was away, every day Mac made his way to the stream to drink, and then went on to the cottage to eat.

On their return home, the children's father made a fuss of him, and, for his benefit, his wife and children feigned

interest in him too.

Mac sensed an air of excitement amongst them, but couldn't make out what it was until, a day or two later, he overheard the children's parents talking about moving house, across to the other side of the country, to Dublin.

It seemed that, following the father's very successful business trip overseas, he had been offered promotion to a better paid position in the firm's Dublin office, to be part of the team in charge of the company's overseas operation.

The move was not to take place immediately, and, in the interim, the children's father would be dividing his time between the demands of his existing job, and those of the Dublin office. He was to be kept very busy indeed.

For the next three months, Mac very rarely saw the children's father. He would come home for an overnight stay every ten days or so, but would be away again very early the next morning.

It was during this time that, to Mac's alarm, the indifference of the children and their mother towards him began to turn into open hostility, with each of them actively discouraging him from coming anywhere near them, or the house. He was not fed, he was barred from entering the house, and the children chased him out of the garden whenever they saw him.

No longer being offered any sustenance of any kind at home, he had come to rely entirely upon the stream for water, and the bird table at the cottage for food.

Unknown to Mac, inside the house the children's mother was busily sorting and packing her family's belongings.

She was preparing for their removal to Dublin, and early on in her preparations, she had decided that there was no way in the world Mac was going to go with them. She saw the move as an opportunity to be rid of him, for good.

Not knowing what else to do, after drinking from the stream and eating at the cottage, each day Mac returned to his home, but took care to stay out of sight. There, he watched and waited to see what would be the outcome of it all.

He didn't have too much longer to wait because, early one morning, a removal van arrived. It was parked close to the house, its rear doors opened, and then two men spent the remainder of the morning going in and out of the house, collecting packing cases and furniture, which then were loaded into the van.

As far as he could see, the children's father was not present, and so Mac did not approach, opting instead for watching and waiting for him to arrive.

He didn't come, and the last Mac saw of the family to whom he had been entrusted,was the mother shepherding the two children into the back seat of the car, before climbing into the driver's seat, and then, without a backward glance, driving the car away.

With the removal van having left shortly before the family, all was then quiet and deserted.

Not believing the children's father would have abandoned him, timidly Mac approached the house, to see if he might have arrived unnoticed, and was inside. He peered in through each of the windows in turn. He saw that all the rooms had been completely stripped of their contents, and the whole place was empty and deserted.

It was when Mac discovered his bed had been discarded next to the wheelie bin, awaiting collection for disposal with the rubbish, that he sat down, burst into tears, and sobbed as if his heart would break.

He didn't care about the others, but now he believed that the children's father, his only friend in that household, had forsaken him too.

Sadly for Mac, he didn't know that his friend had not

knowingly abandoned him, and never would have done so. In fact, what had happened was that, having successfully driven Mac away from his home, whenever the children's father was at home overnight, the children and their mother had been telling him that Mac had mysteriously disappeared. His wife had told him that she and the children had searched everywhere for him, but couldn't find him, and she believed he had been knocked down and killed on the road.

Having no reason to doubt his wife's word, he had accepted what she had told him, and, on his family joining him at their new home in Dublin, he had had no idea whatsoever that Mac had been abandoned and was alone, frightened and distressed, at their former home 200 miles away in Kerry.

It was well into the afternoon before Mac dried his tears, and left.

He drank at the stream, and then ate at the cottage, before beginning to look for somewhere to spend the night.

While the family had still been at the house, as soon as it was dark, he had been sneaking into an outhouse to sleep each night, but now he never again wanted to go anywhere near the place where he had been so unhappy.

The family had shown him that he was unloved, and unwanted, and so now, somehow, he would have to make a new life for himself, on his own.

A short distance downstream from the cottage, he found a dense group of furze bushes, and, crawling along carefully on his belly, he found he could just squeeze his body under the lower branches, and, with some difficulty, he managed to avoid the sharp prickles above him, and made his way into a dry, bare area of earth near to the centre of the group.

Given the trauma of the day he had just endured, he slept surprisingly well, and, at the break of day the next day, he crawled out from his overnight refuge.

He was surprised to see the surrounding vegetation was glistening with raindrops.

It was very wet underfoot, and obvious there had been heavy rain at some time during the night. His furze sanctuary though had remained dry and snug, and he was surprised at the discovery that the bushes could be so impenetrable to rain.

That augured well for making his overnight refuge a more permanent home because, as well as being convenient for water and food, now it had shown itself to be dry, warm, and relatively comfortable.

For the next two months, Mac made his home under the furze bushes, drank from the stream, and ate at the cottage.

He was lonely, but at least he had water to drink, food to eat, and somewhere safe to sleep.

He didn't want to spend the remainder of his life on his own, but he could see no other alternative, and, gradually, he became accustomed, and resigned, to his lonely lifestyle, envisaging and accepting, as he did, that it was to be all life would have to offer him for the rest of his days.

In all probability that indeed would have been so, had fate not then taken a very unexpected turn.

Deception

During the time Mac had been with the family, whenever the children's father had seen Orla's father, and had been asked about Mac, innocently he had related the situation for Mac in his family as he saw it, and had reassured him that all was well with Orla's friend.

On the last occasion he saw Orla's father, immediately before the family's move to Dublin, he hadn't had the heart to tell him that Mac was missing, and was believed to be dead, and so he allowed him to think that Mac was going to be moving house with them.

After that, having no reason then to go to Cork in the course of his job, he never contacted Orla's father again, and so it was that both Orla's parents remained in ignorance of what had actually happened during Mac's stay with that family.

It was as well for them that they didn't know, because it would have made the grief for their little daughter even harder for them to bear.

Moving On

When Mac arose from his earthen bed that morning, everything seemed to be just the same as usual, and he set off from his home, to follow the monotonous routine his daily life had become.

He drank his fill from the stream, and then trotted on to the cottage. As usual, the place was quiet and deserted.

It was once he was around in the rear garden that he was astounded by what then came into view.

At the top of the pole, immediately below the platform, a wide umbrella of mesh had appeared, and, to Mac's dismay, he knew that even Sidney himself wouldn't be able to negotiate such an obstacle.

Unknown to Mac, although the woman who lived in the cottage had never actually seen him, she had discovered the scratch marks from his claws on the pole, and, when the food she put out for the birds kept mysteriously disappearing, she had assumed the culprit to be the animal who had left the marks, and so had invested in a "baffle" to prevent its access on to the platform.

Mac stared in misery at the baffle and then at the food which was now beyond his reach.

Even with so little hope of finding any food elsewhere on the property, nevertheless he searched every nook and cranny, but, as he had anticipated, there was nothing. He left, and returned to his home in the furze bushes.

There, he remained for the remainder of the day, feeling anxious, frightened, and very hungry.

He slept very little that night. He was too worried. He knew that without a source of food available to him, he couldn't stay, and he would have to move on.

That prospect filled him with fear. He had had no experience of permanently fending for himself in the wild, and he had very serious doubts about his ability to do so. Nevertheless he knew he would have to try.

The next morning, he set off early. He drank from the stream, and, in the vain hope that the situation might have changed at the cottage, he went there to check.

Nothing had changed. The baffle was still firmly in place, and the food was still inaccessible to him.

He turned, and left.

He knew he was in trouble, and, remembering old Phyllis' words, he shaded his eyes against the sun and scanned the surrounding countryside. Unfortunately for Mac, there was not a pheasant to be seen. He was on his own.

For the remainder of the morning, he followed the course of the stream as it meandered its way down the hillside, away from the cottage and his furze home, until it disappeared underground.

He looked around, and saw that in front of him were fields bounded by old stone walls, bushes and trees, but there was no food anywhere to be seen.

It was while he was standing there, trying to decide what to do next, that something hit him, very hard.

He was knocked to the ground. He tried to get up, but

was hit again, knocking him over on to his back, and it was then he found himself looking up into the face of a large and fearsome looking all black tomcat who was standing over him.

The cat's eyes were narrowed into slits, his lips were drawn back from gleaming white teeth, and he was flexing the razor sharp claws of the paws with which Mac was being held down.

Mac was too frightened to move.

The tomcat hissed menacingly as he spat out the words to Mac, "You ….. you clear off."

Then the cat paused, to shove his face down close to Mac's, before going on, "Get out. Understand?"

Never before had Mac been attacked by one of his own kind. He didn't know it happened, and he didn't know what to do. He was trembling with fright, and was too terrified of this menacing stranger to be able to speak.

In any event, the tomcat didn't wait for an answer, settling instead for hitting Mac again, hard.

Still Mac didn't speak or move. He didn't know how to defend himself, and, in his confusion and fear – and although he had no idea then, or afterwards, why he did so – he started to purr.

To his surprise, this startled the tomcat. He jumped back away from Mac, and, staring at him in disbelief, he shouted at Mac, "What's the matter with you? I can really hurt you, you know."

Mac was still too frightened to speak, but, seeing the effect of his purring upon the tomcat, he kept it going, louder and louder.

The tomcat was the local bully, and he had been accustomed to those he picked upon trying to run away from him. He'd never had one purr at him before! This one must be some kind of lunatic, and that made him nervous. He hesitated, and then decided to give Mac a wide berth.

He continued to back away from Mac and, when well away from him, he shouted back to Mac, "Remember what I've said ….. you clear off, you, you lunatic. You stay away from me or, or, it'll be the worse for you, you see." Then he turned, and fled.

Shakily, Mac rose to his feet, and then examined his wounds. The edges of both of his ears were torn and bleeding, there was a deep cut on his left shoulder, and he had bad grazes on his knees and elbows from being knocked so hard to the ground. He stretched each of his limbs in turn, and, although they felt very sore, there didn't seem to be any serious, permanent damage.

Judging from the expression on the tomcat's face as he retreated, Mac felt fairly confident that he would not be troubled by him again.

Looking about him, the tomcat was nowhere to be seen, and so Mac continued on his way.

He had walked for a while before the stream re-emerged from underground and continued on above ground. He could see that in the near distance the stream widened and that there was a thick hedge beside it on his side of the water, beyond which, in the far distance, there was a high stone wall. He thought it might be difficult to negotiate past these two potentially formidable obstacles to his progress and so decided he had best cross to the other side of the stream while he had the opportunity to do so at the point immediately above where it surfaced.

Once across, he sat at the stream's edge, watching the cool water bubbling up from underground. It was then he realized he was very thirsty, and so drank his fill, before dabbing the cooling water on to his wounds, which were beginning to feel hot, and were stinging badly.

It was as he sat there, he noticed a cat approaching. His heart began to thump with apprehension of it perhaps being his attacker returning, but, as the cat came closer, he saw that he was young, about his own age and size, and well turned out in an immaculately groomed black and white coat.

As the stranger drew level with him, he smiled, and spoke.

"Hello," he said, and then, noticing Mac's injuries, asked, "are you all right?"

"Yes, yes," said Mac, "it looks worse than it is."

Nevertheless, the stranger looked concerned as he went on, "What's happened to you ..... have you had an accident?"

"No," said Mac, "not an accident, a big black tomcat attacked me ..... he told me to 'clear off', but I've nowhere to go."

"Ah," said the stranger, "I think I know that cat ..... when I was very small I had lost my mother and I asked him if he had seen her, but he told me to 'clear off' too and then hit me and hurt me," he frowned, "he can be very unpleasant."

"Oh," said Mac, "I see, it's not just me then."

"Mind you," said the stranger, "after I went to live at The Bothy with Felix and Fionn ….. he's a huge dog you know ….. he's never come near me since. Too scared of Fionn ….. you see, bullies are like that."

The young cat grinned, and then said, "Actually, Fionn wouldn't hurt a fly ….. " He stopped and laughed, before continuing, "but the tomcat doesn't know that ….. and we're not telling him!"

"Oh," said Mac, "that's good."

"Now," said the stranger, "I'm forgetting my manners. I should have introduced myself. I'm Korky."

"And I'm Mac ….. or Mr. Mac ….. I had a friend once who called me that." said Mac wistfully.

"Well, Mr. Mac," said Korky, "may I ask to where you are headed?"

"Oh, I don't know," said Mac miserably, "somewhere, anywhere, nowhere, I just don't know."

"Are you in trouble?" asked Korky.

"Yes, I am," said Mac, "my people have gone away and left me behind and, and," his eyes began to fill with tears, "I don't know what to do, or where to go."

"Now, now" said Korky sympathetically, "don't upset yourself, I'll help you."

"How?" asked Mac.

"Well, when I was little and injured, Felix ….. oh I should have said that Felix is a black and white cat, like me ….. Felix rescued me, and took me home to live with him and his friend, Fionn, and I'm sure he will help you too."

"Do you think he would?" asked Mac anxiously.

"Yes, I'm sure of it ….. " he smiled as he went on, "and

I think the sooner I get you to him, the better, because those wounds of yours might need attention to stop them getting infected."

"Well, if you're sure it would be okay ….. " said Mac, slowly.

"Yes," said Korky, "I'm absolutely sure ….. and anyway you would be doing us a favour," his eyes twinkled, "you see, we're short of a wicket keeper for cat cricket."

Cat cricket? Mac had never heard of such a thing.

Korky saw the puzzled expression on Mac's face and grinned, saying, "I'll tell you all about cat cricket and 'The Felcans' when we get there."

With that, he said, "Follow me." then turned and set off back in the direction from whence he had come, with Mac apprehensively following on behind.

Korky led his new friend downhill beside the stream and they had not gone far before they came to a gate, beyond which there was a *bóithrín*, deeply rutted with tractor tracks.

Leading the way to squeeze under the gate's bottom bar, Korky said, "C'mon Mac, under here."

Mac followed him, and, once through, he saw the way ahead stretched away into the distance beside the stream. On the opposite side of the *bóithrín*, there was a sod and stone bank, with a thick growth of ferns and wild flowers, topped by a row of blackthorn bushes.

The cats continued on their way, and, after having gone some considerable distance, Mac saw the remains of an old gateway coming into view, and on his right, the start of a very high old stone wall. They walked on and Mac was surprised to see the very high old stone wall give way suddenly to the whitewashed wall of a long, old farmhouse with a roof of thatch above.

He was about to ask Korky about it, when Korky stopped and pointed at the building, saying, "That's it, Mac, that's The Bothy ….. we're here."

Mac saw there was a row of seven small windows set into the wall, but could see no door, and, just as he was wondering how they would get into it, Korky spoke again. "From here, we have to go around to the front gates to get into the yard."

Mac followed Korky down the *boíthrín* beside the farmhouse, before Korky then turned right on to the *bán* of the old farmhouse. He saw that where the *bán* met the lane beside the farmyard, the stream disappeared underground again.

As he and Korky then squeezed under the old iron gates into the farmyard, Mac saw that to his left was fuchsia hedging above an old stone wall which abutted a long, low stone built barn. At right angles to that building was another smaller one. Immediately opposite the barn was the front of the old farmhouse. He noticed that fast asleep on a comfortable looking bed close to the wall of the old farmhouse to his right, was a large, mid-grey coloured Great Dane dog, and then, just coming into view was a very large black and white cat, who was emerging from the doorway of the barn to the left of the farmyard. He appeared to be elderly, but his bearing was that of a much younger cat, and, despite his greying temples and muzzle, he was still handsome.

Beckoning to Mac to follow him, Korky ran across the

yard to the old cat. "Felix," said Korky, "this is Mac, he's in trouble, and he needs our help."

Felix smiled indulgently at Korky, and, turning to Mac, said, "I'm Felix, and of course we will be happy to help you in any way we can."

"Thank you." said Mac.

"Now," said Felix cheerily, "you tell me all about it."

Before Mac could speak, Korky launched enthusiastically into telling Felix all that Mac had told him, ending with, "and can he come to live with us?"

Felix smiled, "Well, Korky, that depends upon whether Mac wants to live here with us."

He turned to Mac, and asked him.

"Yes," said Mac, "I would very much like to live here, if that's all right with you."

Felix smiled again, "Yes, and I know I'm speaking for Korky and old Fionn too, when I say you are most welcome to join us."

A thought occurred to Mac, "But what about the people in the farmhouse, will it be all right with them?"

"Oh yes." said Felix, "There are no worries on that score, I've known Cara and Abe for years and years, and they never turn away any animal in need ..... they'll be quite happy to have you here."

Korky looked from Felix to Mac, and then, smiling happily, he said, "So that's settled then." He was so looking forward to having a companion of his own age.

"Yes." said Felix to Korky, and then to Mac, "Come along indoors and have something to eat, you must be very hungry."

"Yes, thank you," said Mac, "indeed I am. I've had nothing to eat since the day before yesterday."

After Mac had eaten, Felix examined his wounds. The blood had dried and Felix told him that they looked clean and he thought it probable they would heal well left alone, but when Cara came with their tea later on, he didn't doubt she too would examine them and, if she thought they needed treatment, she would see to it.

After his ordeal of being attacked, no sleep the previous night, and his long walk that day, now that he felt safe and had eaten, suddenly Mac felt utterly exhausted.

Felix and Korky were keen to hear more about him, and, not wanting to offend his benefactors, Mac did his best to stay awake, but it was when he just couldn't stifle a wide yawn, that Felix noticed he was exhausted.

"Now Mac," he said, "you must rest, everything else can wait until later."

"He can use my bed." said Korky, eager to do his bit to help his new friend.

"Yes, thank you, Korky," said Felix, "that's a good idea for now, and then, later on, we can get another bed ready for Mac."

Mac sank down gratefully on to Korky's bed, and, as he drifted off into sleep, he heard Felix saying, "You have a good sleep, and later on, when he's awake, we'll introduce you to Fionn."

"Yes, thank you," said Mac sleepily, "I would like that." and, seconds later, he was deeply asleep, happily dreaming of Orla.

Another New Friend

Mac slept soundly until teatime.

He awoke to the sound of a human voice.

He opened his eyes and saw a woman standing nearby. She was talking to Felix and Korky. Setting down two dishes of food, she said to them, "Well now, you two, here's your tea."

Korky and Felix purred as she told them they were good cats and stroked each of them on the head.

It was as she turned to leave that she noticed Mac.

She spoke to Korky and Felix again, "Well, there's a surprise. Now who is this?"

She answered her own question. "A friend of yours I don't doubt."

Korky and Felix purred in agreement.

With that, she said, "Hello." to Mac and told him to wait there while she fetched him some tea too.

She turned and left, re-appearing a few minutes later, carrying a dish of food for Mac.

Mac approached her timidly, and purred his thanks.

It was then that Cara noticed Mac's injuries and, as Felix had predicted, she examined them.

Felix felt pleased with himself when Cara confirmed his own opinion that they were clean and safely could be left to heal on their own.

With one last look at the three cats, Cara told them to enjoy their meal, and then left, leaving the barn door ajar behind her.

"C'mon," said Felix to Mac, "tuck in."

Mac sampled the food, and, despite having eaten only a few hours earlier, it was so delicious that, in no time at all, he had eaten every scrap.

Korky and Felix had been eating steadily too, but, being accustomed to having good food available to them every day, they left some to eat later.

Silence had reigned while they ate, but, when the three cats had finished eating, Felix suggested that he and Korky take Mac to meet Fionn, who, by now, would be waking up.

Felix was right. Fionn was stirring from sleep as the three cats crossed the yard towards him.

Felix approached first, and tapped one of his old friend's paws gently, saying, "Fionn, are you awake? There's someone here I'd like you to meet."

Still with his eyes closed fast, Fionn grunted and said, "Yes, what is it? What do you want?"

Felix turned to Mac, and explained that Fionn's hearing was not so good nowadays.

Then he lifted the flap of one of Fionn's ears, and shouted into the ear, "There's someone here for you to meet."

"All right, all right," grumbled Fionn irritably, "there's no need to shout, I'm not deaf."

Felix smiled and whispered to Mac, "He won't admit he's hard of hearing."

Fionn opened his eyes. "Now," he said to Felix, "what's all the fuss about?"

"No fuss," said Felix, "I just want you to meet Mac ….. he's come to live with us."

"Who's come to live with us?" queried Fionn.

"Mac." said Felix.

"Who's Mac?" asked Fionn.

"That's what I've come to tell you ….. he's come to live with us."

"Well, why didn't you say so in the first place?"

"I did."

"No you didn't."

"Yes I did."

"No you didn't."

Korky smiled at Mac. Korky was used to these two old friends bickering about who had said what, to whom.

Korky intervened.

"Fionn," he said, bringing Mac forward, "this is my new friend, Mac ….. say 'Hello' to him."

"Ah," said Fionn to Korky, "some sense at last, now I

know what's going on."

He smiled at Mac. "Hello," he said, "you mustn't mind us old fogies, we get into a bit of a tangle with each other sometimes. He's a bit deaf you see," he paused, before conceding, "it's our age too, of course, not as alert as we used to be ….. " then he grinned widely at Felix, "but we're great friends really, aren't we Felix?"

Felix smiled fondly at his old friend, "Yes, we go back a long way, and a lot has happened in that time."

"Now," said Fionn to Mac, "what brought you here?"

Before Mac had the chance to speak, once again Korky launched enthusiastically into telling Mac's story.

When he had finished, Fionn said, "Well Mac, after all you've been through, I hope you will be very happy here with us ….. you deserve to be."

"Thank you, Fionn," said Mac quietly, "you are all being so very kind to me, and I don't know what I would have done without your help."

"Think nothing of it," said Fionn, "we're pleased to have you here, and it will be good for Korky to have someone of his own age around ….. " his eyes twinkled, "he never says so, but I'm sure he gets fed up with just us two oldies for company."

"Well," said Felix to Fionn, "now that's sorted out, I guess we'd best leave you in peace."

"Yes," said Fionn, "it's beginning to get a bit chilly now, and anyway it's just about time for me to go in for my tea."

The three cats stood back, as, slowly, Fionn rose to his feet.

Once at his full height, Mac was totally overawed by his immense size. He found it difficult to believe that any dog could be that big. Fionn was taller than either Primrose, or Jasmine, when he first knew them. Then he smiled to himself as the thought crossed his mind as to what Murphy would have made of meeting a dog of this size.

It was then Mac realized he was staring at Fionn, but, fortunately, none of the others had noticed.

Before heading for the door of the farmhouse, Fionn turned to Mac and said, "Felix and Korky will look after you tonight, and I'll see you again in the morning ..... sleep well."

"Yes, thank you," said Mac politely, "and I look forward to seeing you again tomorrow."

With that, Fionn wished them all goodnight, and, as he started off for the door of the farmhouse, the door was opened from the inside.

Fionn paused for a moment in the doorway, to wish them all goodnight again, and then went indoors.

Almost immediately, Cara came out, and she smiled at the three of them, before collecting Fionn's bed, and taking it indoors.

The cats returned to the barn and, after preparing a bed for Mac for later, that evening they sat together and chatted.

Mac reminded Korky that he had promised to tell him all about cat cricket.

Korky was anxious to impress his new friend with his knowledge of the game, and so happily launched into a long and detailed description and explanation of how it was played.

He told Mac that it had been introduced into the area long, long ago by an elderly English cat, and had been played there ever since. He explained that its popularity lay in its flexibility, in that it could be adapted to suit any number of players, and so no-one ever need be left out because of too many, or play suspended because of too few.

"When I came here," said Korky, "Felix hadn't played for years and years, but then he and Fionn revived it for me." He smiled, "It was very good of them really, because, as you can see, they're no longer young, and keeping a little, energetic kitten amused was really hard work for them," he smiled again, "but then they got to enjoy it too."

"It must be great fun." said Mac.

"Yes," said Korky, "it is."

Korky kept chattering on about the number of games they had played and of how he, Felix and Fionn had decided to call themselves 'The Felcans'.

All the while, Felix sat by, quietly observing the two young cats as they chatted and laughed together. He had long been concerned that the youthful Korky had had only himself and old Fionn for company, and he could hardly believe his good fortune to have had his prayers answered by the arrival of Mac. Korky would now have a companion of his own age to share his life.

Silently, he thanked their Lord Provider for guiding Mac into their lives.

Judging from his demeanour, Mac very obviously had been well brought up, and so he was sure he would be a good influence on Korky. He was polite, and respectful, and, despite all the hardship he had endured at the hands of uncaring people, his own kind and caring disposition still shone through.

Felix was certain that Mac and Korky would be great friends and that their friendship would benefit each of them.

Late into the evening, Korky and Mac continued chatting and laughing together, and they were so engrossed in each other's company, that it was Felix who, with some reluctance, eventually made the decision it was time for all of them to retire to bed.

It was not until then that Mac realized just how much such an eventful day had taken out of him, and, suddenly, he felt so very, very tired.

As they made for their beds, Mac had tears in his eyes when he said quietly to the other two, "You know, I really can't thank you enough for what you're doing for me."

Korky smiled, and Felix told their new friend that he was very welcome.

And so passed the first day of what promised to be a happy new life for Mac at The Bothy.

The Bothy

Felix's barn stood across a concreted yard from an old stone and thatch farmhouse.

The barn was about 12 metres long and in the front wall towards one end was a stable door opening out on to the yard, and, at the other end, double doors, which led out into the second of two small fields.

Attached to the barn, at a right angle and facing the yard, was an old animal house, which also had a door opening out on to the yard.

High up and set at intervals around the thick stone walls of both buildings were unglazed slit windows, which both ventilated the buildings and let in the light.

At the end of the old animal house was a gate into the second field, and, on the side of the yard immediately opposite, were old iron gates to the lane outside.

The land behind the barn was at a higher level than that of the yard and, through a gap in wild fuchsia hedging, stone steps from the yard led up into that field – which was divided from its neighbour only by willow trees and thick bushes beside a shallow ditch. A gate, hung from a stone pillar built into the back wall of the barn, led into the second field.

At first, the field to the rear of the barn was flat, but then began to slope downwards until, at its lowest point, it was divided from the remainder by a large pond, to one side of which was a boggy area with an extensive growth of fragrant meadowsweet, and, to the other, an expanse of wild yellow 'flag' irises. The iris end of the pond was overlooked by a grassy bank extending down from the higher level of the second field, and which, in Spring, was clothed in the delicate yellow of primroses in bloom.

The pond narrowed in the centre and it was there that access across it to the rest of the field was gained by way of a bridge of rock, comprising of three enormous boulders – one at each side, and a longer, flatter one than either of the others spanning the water between the two.

A path then led away from the pond uphill towards the headland, winding its way up through rough grass and bracken, to meet the beginning of an old path which was enclosed on both sides by the remains of old stone walling, over which tumbled a thick growth of wild woodbine.

To the left of the old path was a small copse of whitethorn and blackthorn trees, beyond which was another field, lying between the trees and the lane which had first passed by the front gates of The Bothy's yard, on its way down to the harbour and the pier, where local fishermen moored their boats and landed their catches of fish.

In the area to the right of the path, the bracken extended uphill until stopping abruptly at the edge of where the headland ended at an escarpment of rock which fell away steeply down to the seashore far below, where its boulders spilled out haphazardly over the pebbles and sand.

The second field at the homestead was comprised of more pasture, and less bracken, but on its seaward side

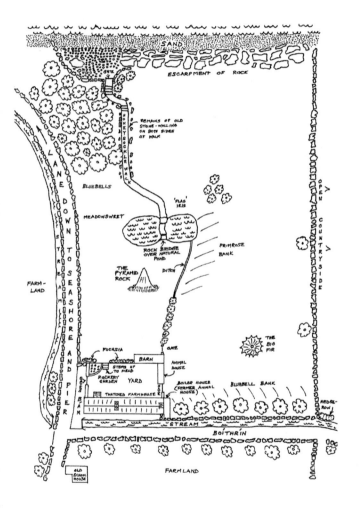

similarly ended abruptly at the steep rocky escarpment.

The only way down on to the seashore from either field was by way of the old path on the part of the headland which sloped away north-westwards.

At the end of the path, there descended a short flight of stone steps, followed by a corner turning to the left, and another longer flight of steps down to a small area shaded by a large whitethorn tree, and a gate.

Beyond the gate was the seashore.

Locally, the path was known variously as the honeysuckle, or woodbine, walk.

Getting To Know A New Home

The next morning, after breakfast, Korky offered to show Mac around The Bothy.

Felix smiled to himself as he watched the two of them leave the barn together. Korky was chattering on so happily to his new friend, with Mac listening and nodding, it was obvious to anyone that Mac wasn't getting much of a chance to speak.

Felix was delighted to see Korky so happy. He remembered the tiny lost, frightened and distressed kitten he had found and had brought home to nurture, and of how he had had to wait until Korky was a lot older before he could admit to him his belief that the kitten's mother had been killed on the road, and so he would not see her again in this life. Even then, he had cried, and Felix had had to comfort him.

He smiled again as he thought of all the difficulties he had faced, and of all the mistakes he had made because of being an old bachelor trying to raise a very young kitten on his own.

Well, not quite on his own, because Fionn had done what he could to help, but of course he had never been a kitten himself and so knew very little about them, or their needs. He remembered how, at times, he had even wished it had been a puppy he had rescued, so that he could have handed over to Fionn the bulk of the anxiety and the weight of responsibility of the upbringing of one so very young.

Still, after all the problems and hard work, he had been rewarded handsomely with an intelligent, cheerful and exceptionally amiable youngster, of whom anyone would be proud.

He was so very proud of his protégé, and now, at last, Korky had company of his own age, that indeed was a blessing. He had been worried about Korky's future with only two old fogies for company, and now that was a worry no more because when he and Fionn were no longer around, Korky would not be alone. He was certain Korky and Mac were destined now to be lifelong friends.

He saw Korky pointing to the thatched roof of the farmhouse, and knew he was telling Mac all about how he, Felix, had become stuck on the roof when he was young and had had to be rescued. It had been Felix who had told Korky the tale of his less than successful climbing exploit all those long years ago.

"And so," said Korky to Mac, "can you just imagine it, there's Felix, all small and frightened, clinging for dear life to the chimney pot, and refusing to try to climb down because he's sure he will fall."

Mac smiled to himself. He was having difficulty imagining the imposing figure of Felix as a small kitten.

Korky went on, "And then, Cara persuades him to try to climb down, he falls, lands on her, knocks her backwards, and they both roll down off the tin roof and hit the ground."

He laughed, "She's lying there, winded, and Felix thinks he's killed her."

Mac conjured up a mental picture of the scene, and laughed too.

Anxious then to continue his tour, Korky said, "C'mon, Mac, through the gate, and I'll show you the Big Fir."

Then the two boys were at the foot of the big old tree, and Korky was telling Mac all about how Felix, the ever intrepid kitten, managed to get himself stranded up that too, and had to be rescued.

Mac was beginning to think that there was much more to Felix than met the eye.

Next, the two boys were scrambling up to the top of the old stone wall of the back field, to peer over it at the open countryside beyond.

Korky said to Mac, "You see the way the land drops away from the other side of this?"

"Yes," said Mac, "what about it?"

"Well," said Korky, "when Felix was very little, he was following a pheasant and fell down that side of the wall to the bottom, and couldn't get back again."

"Oh dear," said Mac, "what happened?"

"Well, he tried to find another way back home ....." Korky saw that Mac was trying to picture a miniature version of Felix, trudging along on fat little legs, and grinned, saying, "Yes, it's hard to picture him as ever being tiny, isn't it?"

Mac smiled, "Yes, it is."

"Well, he was, and he searched and searched for a way back, but it took him until the next day to find his way to the *boíthrín*, ... you know, the one we used ..... and to get back home that way."

"Didn't the pheasant help him?" asked Mac.

"No, there was someone shooting at the pheasant, and he flew away ….. " Korky looked perplexed, "and anyway, why would a pheasant help a cat?"

Mac smiled wryly, "No reason," he said, "except it made me think of Phyllis."

"Phyllis?" asked Korky, "Who's she?"

"Old Phyllis was my friend," said Mac, "and she was very kind and understanding to me when I was little."

"Oh no, I don't believe it," said Korky, "now you're going to tell me that Phyllis is a pheasant ….. am I right?"

Mac grinned, "You are indeed." he said.

Korky had never even seen a pheasant, let alone met one, and so he was very curious.

"Tell me," he said to Mac, "what are they like ….. what was Phyllis like?"

"Well," said Mac wistfully, as he remembered the friend from his kittenhood, "Phyllis was old, and a bit grumpy, but she had lots of stories to tell about life in the wild wood," he laughed, "but she didn't approve of Deirdre and me wasting energy on playing games ….. or 'hi jinks', as she called them."

"Deirdre," asked Korky, "who's she?"

"Oh, she was a young deer I used to play tag with in the woodland," he smiled, "well, come to think of it, perhaps it was not much of a game for me, because she could run and dodge in and out of the trees so fast, I could never catch her."

Mac fell silent, and thought about his friends, before saying quietly, "Then of course there was Sidney, the squirrel, Primrose and Jasmine, the calves, and their mothers, Daisy and Bluebell, and then of course old Murphy, the donkey."

"You seem to have had a very strange collection of friends ..... didn't you know any cats?" asked Korky.

"No, none around ..... " said Mac, "except for my parents of course. You see, I didn't have any brothers and sisters, so there were no other kittens to play with."

"Oh," said Korky, "like me then, when there was just Mamma and me," his voice faltered as he went on, "and then ..... and then, something happened to her, and I was on my own."

"I'm so sorry," said Mac, "that must have been awful for you."

"Yes, it was," agreed Korky, and then he smiled, "but then Felix found me, and brought me here." He was thoughtful for a moment, before smiling again and saying, "I was very lucky really because first I had the very best Mamma in the world, and then, when she was gone, Felix took me in and brought me up."

"That was very kind of him," said Mac thoughtfully, "I think there would not be too many of his age willing to care for and raise a very young kitten."

"No," said Korky, "and it was not easy for him because I was so very little and I was injured, and," his eyes shone with admiration for his benefactor, "I was very distressed over losing my Mamma ..... I missed her so much, I cried a lot."

"Yes, I can understand that." said Mac quietly.

"But," said Korky, "he cared for me and comforted me,

and got me through it all. Without him I would have died ….. I have a lot for which to be thankful to him."

Korky was quiet for a moment, and then, to lighten the sombre mood, he said cheerfully, "C'mon now, no more dawdling around, there's a lot to show you yet."

With that, he led the way back up the field towards the back of the barn, and then beckoned Mac to follow him through into the front field.

"Now," he said to Mac, "I'll take you down to the seashore."

They set off down the slope towards the pond at the bottom.

Korky stopped on the way, to show Mac the huge pyramid shaped rock just above the pond, saying, "This is one of Felix's favourite spots to sit ….. he likes to sit beside it and doze in the sun." He smiled, "If ever he's missing, this is a good place to look for him."

Korky had no idea at the time that he had just made a profoundly prophetic remark.

As they reached the pond, and started out across the rock bridge, suddenly Korky stopped. He had a funny story to tell Mac.

"Something funny happened here," he grinned, "Fionn told me about it."

"Oh, what happened then?" asked Mac.

"Well, it was when Fionn was much younger than he is now. Before my time of course, but one day Abe was trying to move a big rock across this bridge in one of those wheelbarrow things they use," Korky paused, for maximum effect, "well, half way across, about where we are now, the barrow starts to wobble under the weight, and the rock in it's so heavy it tips the barrow sideways, Abe tries to save it and, and, " Korky began to laugh so much he had difficulty in getting the words out, "next second there's Abe, barrow, and rock, all in the water ….. Abe goes under, and comes up covered in pond weed!"

Mac grinned and said, "Well I never."

"Yes, yes, but you've not heard the best bit yet ….." Korky had to stop again to try to control his laughter, "then, then, there's Cara nearby, she's seen what's happened and runs on to the bridge to help Abe out of the water, then, then," by now Korky was shaking all over with near uncontrollable mirth, with tears running down his face, and he had to stop again before going on, "Fionn's there watching, he goes on to the bridge to get a better look, stands beside Cara, she's still trying to pull Abe out of the water, Fionn's getting caught up in the excitement of the moment, not watching where he's putting his feet and, and," Korky had to stop again, "then, then he slips and falls backwards into the pond on the other side of the bridge!"

At this point in his story, Korky was just about helpless with laughter, "Can you imagine it, there's Cara on the bridge, she's been drenched by the splash of Fionn falling in, Abe's still thrashing about in the water on one side of her, and now there's Fionn floundering in the water on the other side ….. "

Mac could picture it all clearly and started to laugh loudly as Korky went on, "Cara doesn't know what to do, she looks from Abe to Fionn and back again, Fionn's

panicking, too heavy for Cara to help, Abe still struggling, but he can get hold of Cara's hand, so, Abe hauls himself out, nearly pulls Cara in ….. both in a panic about Fionn, but they manage to get hold of him and pull him out ….. crisis over ….. Abe soaked and covered in pond weed, Fionn soaked and covered in pond weed, both standing looking sorry for themselves, Cara soaked too, but starts to laugh, Abe and Fionn see funny side, all three then laughing their heads off ….. "

By the time Korky had reached this, the end of his story, he and Mac were clutching their sides, shrieking with helpless laughter, and, staggering on across the bridge, they collapsed into a heap on the opposite bank.

Neither could speak, but, eventually, when their laughter began to subside, Mac became serious for a moment.

"Do you know, Korky," he said quietly, "this is the first time I've laughed, and felt really happy again, since my friend, Orla, died, and it's all down to you, Felix and Fionn ….. " his voice trembled, "thank you."

Korky smiled, "Think nothing of it, Mac, it's great to have you around."

"Oh," said Mac, "what a wonderful story that was ….. do you really think it's true."

"Yes, positive," said Korky, "just ask Felix, he saw 'em coming back up the field covered in pond weed, and then next day was there when Abe spent the whole of the day trying to get the barrow and rock back out of the pond."

"Did he succeed?" asked Mac.

"Well, sort of ….. he eventually retrieved the barrow, but the rock's still in there, stuck fast in the mud at the bottom ….. too heavy, you see, no shifting that again."

Mac smiled. He knew it was going to be fun living at The Bothy.

"Now," said Korky, "on we go, up the hill, and then I'll show you the only way down the headland to the seashore from here ….. can't get down it from the back field, we'd break our necks if we tried it from there."

Korky led the way up the hill, and then on to the honeysuckle walk, chattering all the way about the seashore beyond.

Mac was quiet. He didn't want to admit to his ignorance. Although he had heard about it, he had never actually seen the sea, so didn't know quite what to expect. His had been inland homes.

Unaware of Mac's embarrassment at not entirely

knowing what he was talking about, Korky continued chattering on happily about the seashore.

Part way along the honeysuckle walk though, suddenly he fell silent, and stopped.

"What is it?" asked Mac.

Korky turned to face Mac, and he looked very serious.

"Just over there," he said, pointing over the wall towards several whitethorn trees, "is my home ….. the one where I lived with Mamma."

"Oh," said Mac, "I see."

"I go there sometimes, and think of her." He looked so sad, Mac didn't know what to say, so said nothing.

Korky went on, "One day I'll take you there to see it ….. but ….. but not today."

Then he smiled at Mac. "Silly of me, it's not a day to be sad for the past, it's a day to look forward to the future."

"Yes." said Mac quietly.

"C'mon then," said Korky, "race you to the end of the walk."

At the end of the walk, they climbed down the two flights of steps, into the cool glade behind the gate. From there, they hopped up and over the wall beside the gate.

Then Mac saw it.

Korky waved his arms first towards one direction, and then the other, saying, "There, there it is, what do you think of it?"

Mac was so overawed, he didn't answer immediately. It was magical, and so beautiful he couldn't believe that it was actually real.

Beyond the pebbles immediately in front of him, and then golden sand, was a huge expanse of silvery blue, shimmering in the bright sunlight.

"So that must be the sea." he thought.

He answered Korky's question. "I think it's the most amazing thing I've ever seen ..... it's wonderful ..... and we can come down here whenever we like?"

"Oh yes," said Korky, "Felix comes down most days for a stroll by the sea, he finds the air bracing, and I often come with him."

"How about Fionn?" asked Mac.

"No," said Korky, "not now, he's quite old and he's worried about the steps ..... such long legs you see, it was okay when he was young, but now he has difficulty with the steps and he's worried he might fall."

"Yes," said Mac, "I can see that, and at his size and weight if he fell down them, he would really hurt himself."

"Hope you will want to come though." said Korky.

"You can bet on that ..... you just try keeping me away." laughed Mac.

Korky said nothing, but he smiled to himself. He was delighted that his new friend liked the seashore he had come to love, and knew so well.

The two cats tiptoed over the pebbles and then wandered along the sand to where Korky wanted to show Mac the dizzy height of the sheer face of rock which rose up to the headland at the seaward end of the back field at The Bothy.

Mac could see how dangerous it would be to attempt either to climb up, or down, it.

Then they retraced their steps, and continued in the

opposite direction, past the gate to The Bothy and around towards the jetty, where Korky had said the local fishermen moored their boats and landed their catches of fish.

They found the jetty deserted, so Korky led the way along to the end of it, crouched down, and peered over.

"Come and see Mac." he cried.

Mac joined him and he too peered down into the clear water.

"Look, there." said Korky.

Mac looked towards where his friend was pointing, and was fascinated to see a shoal of tiny fishes swimming and swirling, as one, this way and that beneath the surface. Tiny silvery darts of life, the like of which Mac had never seen before.

Korky saw the awe on his friend's face.

"That's what I like about it down here," he said, "there's always something of interest to see ….. do you know, just yesterday I saw a seal ….. just swam along a few metres out from me, and kept staring at me ….. you know, with those huge eyes of theirs."

Mac didn't know. He'd never seen a seal, so had no idea what their eyes, or anything else about them, looked like, but he was now very much looking forward to seeing one for himself.

Still not appreciating that Mac knew nothing about the delights of the seashore, Korky continued chattering on, with a mystified Mac just silently nodding in agreement. Suddenly, Korky turned to Mac, and said, "Mmm, time must be getting on by now, so I think we'd best head back. Fionn will be up and about soon and he said he would see you this morning, didn't he?"

"Yes, he did." agreed Mac.

"Well, we don't want to keep him waiting, so is it okay with you if we head back now?"

"Yes, yes," said Mac, "that's fine with me."

Secretly, he felt a bit relieved, because the more Korky talked to him of this strange,and exciting, new world of the seashore, the more he was conscious of his own ignorance of it and ever more anxious not to reveal it to Korky.

The two cats set off for home.

On the way, Korky drew his attention to various points of interest, and, thankfully, most of these were features Mac had seen elsewhere at some time. He knew about furze, fuchsia and holly hedges, and the wild woodbine which covered and draped down the stone walls beside the honeysuckle walk. Even better, when Korky began to talk about the trees which were good for climbing, having had the benefit of Sidney's tuition, that was a subject on which he could enthusiastically converse from a reference point of considerable knowledge and expertise.

Korky was impressed.

At the top of the field, as they approached the steps down into the farmyard, Mac saw that Korky had been right.

Fionn was up and about. He was in the same position as that in which Mac had first seen him the day before – on his bed, close to the wall of the farmhouse. He was resting, and enjoying the mid morning sunshine.

His eyes were closed, but he was not asleep.

The cats approached him, and Korky said loudly, "Fionn, I've brought Mac back to see you ….. " When Fionn didn't answer immediately, he hesitated, before going on, "but we can come back later if you prefer."

Fionn's eyes opened. "No, no, not at all, now's fine."

As the two boys came closer, Fionn looked at both of them intently, saying, "Now you two, come and sit beside me, and tell me all about what you've been doing this morning."

The two boys sat down and Korky began to tell Fionn about their outing to the seashore. Mac joined in where he could, and it didn't take Fionn long to deduce that this had been the first time Mac had ever seen the sea, and he didn't want Korky to know it.

At the end of Korky's description of his and Mac's morning, Fionn turned to Mac and said, "Now Mac, tell me more about yourself."

Shyly, Mac told Fionn all about his parents and his first home, the wonderful life he had had with Orla and her parents, and then of how it had all gone wrong for him, and left him stranded with no home, and no family or friends.

Fionn kept Korky from interrupting, while he listened patiently and sympathetically to what Mac had to say, before asking him, "And now, do you think you can be happy here with us ..... have Felix and Korky been taking good care of you?"

"Oh yes, yes," said Mac, "they've been wonderful to me, I couldn't have asked for better, and ..... and I'm sure I'm going to be very happy here," he paused and lowered his eyes, and then said very quietly, "it's so wonderful to have good friends again."

"Good." murmured Fionn. He thought for a moment and then continued tactfully with, "But I expect our little world here by the sea is a bit different from what you've been used to," his eyes twinkled, "so I think we'll have to make sure that we show you all our own special features here that only we 'locals' know about."

Mac was grateful. He recognized that Fionn had picked up on his ignorance of the seashore and was telling him that if he had any questions about it, he could ask Fionn, in confidence, and so not embarrass himself in front of Korky.

"Yes, thank you," said Mac, "I understand."

"Well," said Fionn, "you two run along now, and I'll see you both later."

As they rose to leave, Fionn looked up at the sky and smiled, "You know, if this weather holds, perhaps tomorrow we can get in a game of cat cricket ….. what do you think, Korky?"

"Oh yes, yes, that would be great." said Korky. He grinned at Mac "And we can enrol you as wicket keeper for 'The Felcans' if you would like that."

"Oh yes," said Mac, "I'm really looking forward to that, but I've never played before you know."

"That's okay," said Korky, "Felix will tell you all you need to know before we begin."

Fionn smiled at them both, "Well then, weather permitting, that's a date ….. so, off you go, I'll need to rest now because I'll need all my energy for tomorrow."

"Race you." said Korky to Mac, and the two boys scampered happily across the yard and into the barn, to tell Felix the good news of the cricket match scheduled for the next day.

The Wicket Keeper

As the day dawned, Mac awoke with a sense of excitement. Today was the day scheduled for his introduction to cat cricket. He felt a little apprehensive too, worrying about perhaps making a fool of himself in front of the others.

He need not have worried.

Just as soon as the three cats had had breakfast, Mac peeped out of the door of the barn, to check the weather, and reported to the other two that it was dry, there was no wind, and there was a cloudless blue sky.

Felix pronounced that to be perfect for cat cricket.

The two boys were anxious to get started, but Felix reminded them that they would all have to wait until Fionn, their only fielder, was up and about and, these days, he did not rise early from his bed.

While they waited, Felix retrieved the bats, ball and wickets from where they had been stored away since the previous Summer. These he showed to Mac, and began to explain to him the rudimentary rules of the game. He explained too that they couldn't even set out the pitch until Fionn was present, as otherwise he would think they had intended to start without him, and that would not do at all.

Both boys waited impatiently for Fionn to appear.

At long last, Fionn appeared in the doorway of the farmhouse.

He called across to Korky and Mac, who had been pacing up and down the yard as they waited.

"Well, it's a lovely day, absolutely perfect for cat cricket ….. are all of you ready, or do you want me to wait a while?"

"No, no," said Korky hastily, "we're all ready, when you are."

"Fine," said Fionn, "you find Felix and then we can set out the pitch."

Felix and Fionn were too old now to walk to any of the past picnic spots of their youth to use as a cat cricket venue as they had in the old days, and, after Korky came into their lives and cat cricket from their younger days had been revived under the name of 'The Felcans', they had settled for the middle (flat) section of the back field on which to stage their matches.

Korky ran into the barn to fetch Felix and, with the two boys carrying the bats, ball and wickets, in no time at all, all four of them were making their way around to the back field.

There, Felix and Fionn directed operations.

Under their instructions, together Korky and Mac drove the stumps of one set of wickets into the soft ground, and then, with Felix counting the paces, they paced out the required 11 cat lengths (including tail), before driving in the stumps of the second set.

Korky nearly forgot the bails, which sent he and Mac scurrying back to collect them from Felix, and each then trotting to opposite ends to rest the bails in place on the stumps.

Fionn and Felix had been flexing their arms and legs, readying them for action, and, at long last, all was ready to begin the game.

Mac took up his position behind the nearest wicket, with Korky in front of him with bat at the ready, and Felix retreating down the field, ready to bowl the first ball.

Korky was anxious to impress Mac with his skill with the bat, and managed to acquit himself quite well, and Mac was to be utterly astonished at Felix's power and accuracy with the ball, and the speed and agility with which Fionn fielded. If this was what they could do in their dotage, they must have been exceptionally formidable opponents in their youth.

Nevertheless, Korky had built up a very respectable score of runs before it was decided it was time for Korky and Felix to exchange places.

Korky bowled with the skill and accuracy Felix had taught him, but his teacher was a formidable opponent, efficiently fending off each ball and keeping Fionn very busy fielding. The pace of the match though had slowed because, although Felix could hit the ball very hard, he could no longer run as fast as had his young opponent, and so his score of runs took rather longer to accumulate.

It was when Felix was totally out of breath, and believed himself unable to run another inch, that a rest break was called.

All four walked slowly off the pitch, to sprawl out on the cool grass behind the old animal house.

During the break, Mac was offered the chance to bat or

bowl when they resumed play, but he declined. In the way that Fionn was content to be permanent fielder, he was perfectly happy to be permanent wicket keeper. It was a position in which he felt there was much less chance of his making a fool of himself.

While he was resting, Mac thought of Phyllis. He felt sure that if she had known cat cricket ever even existed, she would have considered his participation as wasting his energy on foolish things. He hoped though she would have understood how very happy that particular foolish thing was making him, meaning, as it did, his spending a leisurely day in the company of good friends, who cared about him. She too had been a good friend to him, and he wished she could have known his new friends who were now being so good to him too.

They resumed play later on, with Korky back batting, and Felix bowling, and played on late into the afternoon, by which time all four felt very tired, but very happy.

As Felix's efforts had failed to bowl out Korky, Korky's efforts had failed to bowl out Felix, and the combined efforts of Fionn and Mac had not succeeded in running out either, to everyone's satisfaction, the match was declared a draw.

A Glimpse Into The Past

Within a very short time of Mac moving in, he and Korky were scarcely ever to be seen out of each other's company, and Korky diligently, and happily, introduced Mac to all aspects of daily life at The Bothy.

It was a while before Mac asked Korky about the old animal house next door to the barn, which, throughout Mac's time at The Bothy, had been closed up.

What made him ask was that on that particular day, the door had been left ajar, and Mac was curious to know what lay inside.

"It's not that we're not allowed in there," explained Korky, "it's just that no-one lives there any more, and so mostly it's left undisturbed."

He could see Mac was puzzled.

"Well, it was before my time here, but once it was the home of Felix's aunt, cousins, and second cousins, and," Korky looked serious, "it's where Felix's fiancée died, a long, long time ago now."

Mac had wondered why a handsome cat such as Felix must have been in his youth had remained a bachelor, and now this was explained.

"If it's open at any time, you can go in there if you want to, but if you see Felix go in first, don't go barging in, he ….. " Korky paused, "he sometimes sits in there on his own for a while, to remember her, and to feel close to her."

"Oh, I see." said Mac.

Korky went on, "Sometimes too you will see him sitting by the big hydrangea bush next to it ..... that's where she is buried. He likes to sit there quietly, to be with her, so if you see him there, don't disturb him there either."

"Thank you for telling me." said Mac.

Pointing towards the door of the animal house, Korky said, "Felix is in the barn at the moment, so we can go in now to look around if you like, but there's really nothing in there to see."

"No, let's not," said Mac, "it's special to Felix, so let's leave it that way."

Korky agreed.

Friendship and Solace

Not only did Mac find true and lasting friendship at The Bothy, he found solace too for his grief for Orla.

Felix was an old and very wise cat, and, early on, he had recognized that Mac needed help over Orla, and, from his own youthful insight, long long ago now, into what lay beyond the earthly lives of all living creatures, he knew he was in the unique position to give Mac the help he needed.

At every opportunity, Felix encouraged Mac to talk to him about Orla, and, much in the same way as he had reassured Korky about his lost mother, now he reassured Mac that he need have no doubts at all about Orla being safe and very happy in her place beyond the end of the rainbow.

They had long chats together, and Felix told him of how, one day, when Mac's own earthly life was done, he could be sure he would see Orla again, that she would be there waiting for him, and then they could be together, for eternity.

In the meantime, Mac could also be sure that she was watching over him, every minute of every day. Orla loved him and never would she have wanted to have made him so unhappy, so it was his duty now to Orla, his dearest friend, to remember her with joy, not sorrow, because she would be wanting him to enjoy each and every day of the remainder of his earthly life.

Mac knew that Felix would never tell him anything that was untrue, and so it was that Felix's counselling released him from the pain of his grief for Orla, and allowed him the opportunity to live out the remainder of his own life happily and without any feelings of guilt about that happiness.

Although Orla's parents had made a bad mistake when they had sent him away, had they not done so, he would never have met Felix and never had the burden of his grief and longing for Orla lifted from him.

Destiny had brought great unhappiness to him, but also it had taken it away again from him.

Mac wished Orla's parents could have had the benefit of Felix's counselling.

From then on, in the way Felix remembered his fiancée and his family, Mac thought of Orla, but now they were fond memories of the happy times they had spent together and not the sorrow of her passing. He knew now she was not lost to him for ever.

For the rest of his life, every night when he retired to bed, Mac silently thanked their Lord Provider for guiding his steps to the good friends he had found at The Bothy.

He was unaware that every night Korky too thanked their Lord Provider for his similar good fortune, and that Felix and Fionn also offered up their thanks for the blessing of never having known, or having had to endure, the hardship and deprivation to which so many others were subjected during their earthly lives.

Harsh Realities

It was about ten days after the incident of Mac asking about the old animal house, that Korky and Mac happened to be on the rockery garden next to the yard gates, just at the time a battered old vehicle, drawing an equally well worn trailer behind it, and coming from the direction of the jetty, came into view. Just as it was about to pass by the gates, it stopped suddenly.

The boys were curious to know what was going on, and it was as they were about to investigate, that they were startled by a low, gruff voice coming from the trailer.

"Do you know where they're taking us?" it asked.

Korky and Mac scrambled up on to the top of the wall, and then over it, before dropping down on to the edge of one side of the open trailer, to look inside. They were shocked by what they saw.

To their horror, they saw that the trailer was piled high with layers of large live crabs, all packed one on top of another.

A forest of bewildered, anxious eyes were focused upon the two cats.

It was an exceptionally large individual, in the top layer, who was speaking, then telling them his name was Claude, and repeating the question.

"No." answered Korky truthfully, "I'm sorry, I don't."

"Well, we don't like it in here at all. Can you help us?"

Before Korky had the chance to answer, other voices, coming from the depths of the trailer, joined in.

"Is there someone there?"

"Can we get out now?"

"I'm frightened, it's dark and horrid down here."

"What's happened to the sea?"

"I want to go home."

The cacophony of anxious voices, asking for help, confused Korky and Mac, and distressed them too, knowing, as they did, there was nothing they could do to help.

Just at that moment, Cara appeared from nowhere, and, as she approached, the voices fell silent. Puzzled to see the trailer stationary outside the yard gates, she went out and peered into it, just as the driver of the vehicle re-started its engine.

Cara was visibly shocked to see what was in the trailer, and to have all the eyes then focused upon her. So shocked was she by what she saw, she didn't even notice the two cats. The colour drained from her face, her eyes filled with tears, and, as the trailer then began to move off with its cargo of bewildered and frightened prisoners, she turned and hurried away back through the gates, and into the farmhouse.

Korky knew then that Cara couldn't help them either. His heart sank at the prospect that the crabs could be destined for someone's dinner table, and to know that neither he, nor Mac, would ever get to know, or to see any of them again.

As the vehicle gathered speed, and the trailer began to

rock and jolt along the rough surface of the lane, having no other option, Korky and Mac took one last look at the innocent victims of Man's inhumanity towards his fellow creatures, and Korky mumbled, "We're so very sorry." to Claude, before he and Mac hopped down off the trailer, and then slowly made their way back to the yard gates. Neither spoke to the other, both being too distressed to speak of their having had to abandon the crabs to their fate.

As the two boys entered the barn, immediately Felix saw that something was troubling them badly. He sat them down and asked, "Now boys, what's happened? What's wrong?"

Before Mac had the chance to speak, tearfully Korky told Felix about their encounter with the crabs.

Felix's face fell. "Oh dear, I see," he said, "those poor, poor creatures."

Korky said, "I remember when I was very little, you told me that sometimes humans adopted unusual animals as their companions, and that someone famous once kept a lobster as a pet ….." His voice faltered, before asking, "Do you think ….. do you think that Claude and the other crabs could possibly be going to be pets? Er, do you?" His voice trailed off lamely, as he looked expectantly at Felix, his eyes filled with hope.

While recognizing the immediate need was for him to answer Korky's question, Felix made a mental note to speak to him later about the undesirability of humans having wild creatures as pets. He needed to impress upon him that, except in cases of an animal being unable to fend for itself, and therefore in need of human intervention and care to save its life, always wild creatures should be left to live in harmony with Nature, in their natural habitat.

"No, Korky, I'm sorry, but lots and lots of crabs like that will have been caught for one purpose only ….." he paused, and added quietly and gently, "Sadly, they are going to be sold and then cooked for people to eat."

Korky's lip trembled, "Yes, I see ….. I. ….. I thought so ….." He stopped, and then continued, saying, "It's all so horrid, Felix ….. you should have heard them, they were all so frightened ….. and wanting to go back home ….. and ….. and, they were asking us to help them ….." his eyes brimmed with tears, "but …..but there was nothing we could do."

"I know, I know." said Felix, softly, "The sad truth is that there was nothing any of us could have done to save them, and, all the while some humans choose to refuse to accept the truth that Claude and his kind feel pain just as they, and we, do, and continue to want to eat them, that won't change."

Mac said, "We saw that Cara was upset too when she saw them, but, even though she's human herself, I guess she couldn't do anything to help them either."

"No, I'm sure she couldn't." said Felix. "I've known Cara for a very long time, and I know her well enough to know that she will be just as upset and anxious about the crabs."

Mac said, "Yes, she looked very distressed."

"I'm sure she was." said Felix.

He smiled, "I remember one time, long, long ago now, when she came home and found a bucket full of cockles at the door – left by a neighbour for her to cook for Abe to eat." He paused, "But can you guess what she did with them instead?"

"No." said Mac, "What happened?"

"Well, she picked up the bucket and took all the cockles down to the sea and released them back into their home."

Mac smiled.

Korky said nothing, and Felix turned to him and said, "Well, Korky, a bucket of cockles she had been given is one thing, but a whole trailer of crabs in the possession of someone else, sadly, is another."

"Yes, I can see that," said Korky, "but I do wish it had been possible for those poor crabs to have been rescued."

"Yes, I know," said Felix, "and so do we all."

Felix waited, but neither of the boys spoke.

"Well," said Felix, eventually, "while it's all very upsetting for us, we must remember that it's far, far worse for the poor crabs themselves."

Korky looked down at his feet, and mumbled, "Yes, I know."

"What we can do though," said Felix, "is to say a special prayer for them tonight, and ask our Lord Provider to help and protect them through the ordeal they will face before they die."

Felix looked at the boys' glum faces and added, "Now, we must remember too that once their earthly lives have ended, they will all meet up again in peace, safety, and happiness in Newlife, where they will never need to fear anything from anybody, ever again."

He looked intently at both boys, saying, "Now you know I know that to be true, don't you?"

"Yes," said Korky, "and, and I will pray that they are

hurried away quickly into Newlife, to be kept safe from the suffering they will have known in this life at the hands of humans."

He thought for a second or two, and then added, "Why is it, Felix, that some humans do these horrid, cruel things to their fellow creatures, while there are others who would never hurt any of us?"

"That I can't answer, Korky." said Felix. "All I know is that it's always been that way. While there are humans who are kind and think of others, there are some who are ignorant, greedy, selfish, and who are totally indifferent to the needs of others, instead at all times thinking only of themselves. Why those sort were ever allowed into our world is a mystery ….." he paused, "and only our Lord Provider knows why what happens, happens." He paused again, "So, we'll all have to wait until we go into Newlife to get answers to our questions on that score." He smiled, "And for you two boys, that's a very long way off yet."

The boys smiled back, and then made their way to their beds, where they sat together, in quiet contemplation, for the remainder of the evening.

For a long while Felix sat, deep in thought, with a distant look in his eyes. His thoughts were concentrated upon the wild creatures in the world, whose wellbeing, and homes, so often were either at risk, or being threatened by the selfish activities of greedy humans.

Eventually, he came to speak his thoughts aloud, saying, more to himself, than to the boys, "After all, they don't ask for much ….. just to be left alone, to live in peace and safety ….. and yet even that it seems is too much for them to ask of some humans."

The boys nodded, and he continued, "You know, I believe it all stems from humans having appointed themselves as owners of the Earth and assuming a position of power in this world over the rest of us – a power which was never intended to be, and certainly was never deserved."

The boys agreed wholeheartedly, and Felix said no more.

That night all three cats prayed fervently to their Lord Provider for the crabs' speedy deliverance from their suffering. Mac added his own silent plea to his beloved Orla, to take care of them when they arrived in Newlife, and then, content that Claude and his companions would be safe and happy with Orla, he slept peacefully that night.

The plight of the crabs had such a profound effect upon Korky, that, from then on, they continued to feature in his prayers, and he resolved that, however far away that time might be, on the day when, eventually, he entered Newlife, he would seek out Claude and his companions, to explain how he and Mac had not been indifferent to their suffering, and to ask if he could be their friend.

In common with Mac having his motley crew of friends in his kittenhood, Korky saw no barrier to his friendship with the crabs, and, far, far into the future, indeed there would be none.

Friends are friends, whatever species, shape or size they might be. Differences made no difference to true friendship.

The C.C.C.C.C. Inheritance

As time went on, life for those at The Bothy settled into a largely uneventful, but very comfortable, routine of domesticity for all concerned.

Relieved of the responsibility of keeping the youthful Korky occupied and amused, now that he had company of his own age, the elderly Felix and Fionn could relax and take life at a more leisurely pace, much more suited to their advanced years.

It was now that each had the time and opportunity to spend his days quietly in the company of the other, that both began to fully appreciate just how tiring it had been for them to raise a young kitten and keep him active and entertained in order to ameliorate his loneliness for young company. The surprise appearance of Mac into their lives had been a true blessing, for which both elderly animals would remain eternally grateful.

For years now, Felix had applied himself diligently to his co-opted cat role on the Country Creatures Code of Conduct Committee – an hereditary position, sanctioned by the presiding magistrates of the Committee. He had never failed to attend when summoned to do so, and the carefully considered fair and measured opinions he contributed towards the proceedings were very much valued, as indeed his father's similar contribution had been before him.

Two of the three presiding magistrates, Meles the Badger and Lutra the Otter, were very old now, but still mentally alert and well capable of fulfilling the responsibilities their position of authority demanded of them. Sadly, Otus had died some time ago, but, as tradition demanded, an election to select a successor had been held, and Otus had been succeeded by a distant cousin, Tyto, who was himself a mature and very wise owl.

Unknown to anyone at the Bothy – other than his old and trusted friend, Fionn – Felix had petitioned the presiding magistrates to allow Korky to succeed him into his position of co-opted feline on the C.C.C.C.

Felix had explained to them how, as he had grown older, his anxiety had increased about what would happen to his family's ancestral position on the Committee when he died – given that all co-opted positions on the C.C.C.C. traditionally were passed down from father to son. He told them too about how the premature death of his fiancée had denied him the chance of having a son of his own, and it was of great concern to him that the honourable status his family had held on the C.C.C.C. for generations would be destined to die with him.

It was at this point that Felix had drawn in a deep breath, to give him the impetus, and courage, to propose to the magistrates what he had been entertaining in his mind ever since the orphaned Korky had come into his life.

He told the magistrates all about how Korky's mother had been killed by a motor vehicle and of how the brave, and loyal, little kitten had searched for her; how, during his search, he had been attacked and quite badly injured by a local bully, and of how he was close to death from starvation when Felix had found him and taken him in to nurture.

Felix's face had broken into an affectionate smile as he related to the magistrates that during Korky's upbringing at The Bothy, he had come to think of him as his son, and of how he believed that, in the great scheme of things, their Lord Provider had sent Korky to him to fulfil that role in his life. He assured them that Korky was intelligent, respectful, and possessed a strong sense of responsibility and fair play, coupled with kindness towards all his fellow creatures, most particularly those in less fortunate circumstances than himself.

The magistrates had listened patiently, and had anticipated what Felix was about to ask.

In response to the request that special dispensation be granted to allow Korky to succeed to Felix's C.C.C.C.C. position on his death, the magistrates did not give immediate judgement. They told Felix that, as far as any of them was aware, no adopted son had ever succeeded to such a position, but they completely understood his motivation for asking, and would give the proposal very careful consideration.

Having seen the anxiety on Felix's face, and wanting to give him some encouragement, Lutra interjected with, "But just because something hasn't happened before, that doesn't mean it can't ....." he hesitated and looked at the other two magistrates before continuing, "and I, for one would have no objection in principle to an adopted son inheriting ....." he was about to go on, when Meles interrupted him with, "Well, that may be so, but, as we've already agreed, any proposed change to a tradition first needs very careful consideration ….."

Lutra nodded, as Meles then looked intently at Felix and said, "So, Felix, leave it with us to look into the whole question of whether an adopted son may succeed, and indeed Korky's suitability, or otherwise, to succeed you."

Felix had thanked them and had turned to leave, when Meles called after him. "It will take us some time, and a messenger will be sent to advise you of the date for you to return to get our verdict."

Felix felt nervous – today was the day when he would know whether or not Korky could succeed him.

It had been an anxious time of waiting during the intervening weeks, but he had successfully concealed his anxiety from the boys. Outwardly, he had appeared exactly the same as usual, and Korky and Mac remained blissfully unaware of the turmoil of emotions going on inside their benefactor.

Only old Fionn knew, and, whenever the boys weren't around, he and Felix talked long and seriously on the subject. Fionn had wanted to reassure Felix that all would be well, but felt it unwise to do so, because, if the decision of the magistrates went against him, it would make it all the harder for him to accept.

As Felix set off that day to get the long-awaited decision on the future of his family's ancestral C.C.C.C. inheritance, Fionn watched him go with anxious eyes, knowing, as he did, how hard it would be on his old friend were his petition to be refused.

On arrival, Felix waited, in trepidation, before the magistrates.

"Well, Felix," said Meles, "We've come to a decision and I'm sorry it's taken such a long time to do so, but I know you appreciate the importance of what you are asking, and we .....

Unable to stand the suspense, Lutra interrupted impatiently with a fast tumble of words, "What he's trying to say is that we agree your Korky can succeed you ....." He smiled, "there, I've said it."

Meles looked a bit taken aback at the interruption, but then laughed and said, "Well, yes, that's what I was getting around to saying, and, although it's a break with, or perhaps I should say, a variant on, tradition, out of respect for your dear father, and for you, when the time comes, your Korky will be welcomed on to the Committee as your successor."

There were tears of relief and joy in Felix's eyes as he thanked the magistrates profusely, and then left, to hurry away home, to tell Fionn the good news.

He knew now that his hopes would be realized and he could leave a lasting legacy behind him.

He was content.

Over the course of some considerable time, in conversation with Fionn and Korky on his return home from attending meetings of the Committee, surreptitiously he had been preparing Korky for the role he hoped, and now knew, his protégé would play one day in maintaining harmony in the countryside. He knew Korky wouldn't let him down.

Had Felix been able to see into the future, he would have been truly delighted to have seen that indeed Korky did become a respected and worthy member of the Committee, for, just as Felix, and Felix's father, had done before him, he exercised excellent judgement, judgement which, in no small part, was due to his best friend, Mac, who ably assisted him with fair and wise counsel and opinion during his consideration of difficult cases which had been adjourned for decision.

It would also have delighted Felix to have known that, in those circumstances, it was actually *both* of his dear boys contributing to his family's traditional role with the C.C.C.C.

Of Badgers and Men

In fact, Felix's petition to the Committee had come as a timely, and welcome, distraction to Meles, because, at his advanced age, more and more of late he had found himself pre-occupied with gloomy thoughts of the persecution of his own species.

There were the ruthless, cruel thugs who came at night, to terrorise badgers in their homes, and take away members of their family to brutally maim before setting their dogs on them to fight and kill them. Then there were the others, who systematically set about killing whole families of badgers in the mistaken belief they were responsible for making cattle sick.

During his long life, and of being a presiding magistrate of the C.C.C.C.C., several times Meles had witnessed the aftermath of both forms of persecution, and, nowadays, try as he might, he couldn't seem to stop himself dwelling upon the last time it had happened.

He remembered the arrival of the dejected, dishevelled and ragged group of refugees, forced to flee their ancestral home, where generations of the same family had lived for centuries, and which was now lost to them, for ever.

In his mind's eye, he saw, time and time again, that pitiful line of adults, with glazed, unseeing eyes, just stumbling along, one behind the other, with their tearful, bewildered little ones hurrying along beside them, their tiny bodies still trembling with the shock at the horrors they had seen happen at their home.

All had been totally traumatized at having to flee their home, and having to leave behind them the bodies of some of their number.

While they could be provided with temporary housing to keep them comfortable and warm until they could build a new home, Meles knew the psychological damage which had been done to them by such a terrifying experience never would fully heal.

As well as seeking sanctuary, they were wanting answers from him as to why this was happening to them. They simply couldn't understand why it was that they were being accused of making cattle sick.

Meles had tried to explain to them that they were not to blame for anything, and if the humans concerned wanted an answer as to why cattle were getting sick, the cattle themselves knew why. All the while this pogrom against badgers had been going on, the cattle had been desperate to tell the people killing the badgers, that it wasn't they who were making them sick, but the intolerable pressures put on their health and welfare by modern ways of keeping cattle. They gave their all, but still they were asked to give more. Their minds and bodies were exhausted by the pressures put upon them, and that's why they contracted the disease that the badgers were being accused of giving to them.

"But," Meles had told the refugees, "they can't tell them, we can't tell them either, and so it goes on, because humans can't, or won't, see for themselves what's staring them in the face …..tragically, it's a never-ending cycle of undeserved blame, wreaking terrible consequences on cattle and badgers alike."

How it had saddened him that day to know that practical help he could offer, but answers, he had none. There was no way of knowing why it was humans behaved in the way that they did towards their fellow creatures.

He knew from the teachings of the ancients of badger society that, somewhere in the world, always the human race was at war with itself as well, and he had reminded the refugees that humans were equally as ruthless and cruel towards each other, as they were to other creatures. It had always been so, and would remain so, until something could be done about their violent, selfish and greedy inclinations, and their absurd notion that they had been set above all others on Earth, to rule the world.

More to himself than to anyone else, Meles had mused at the time on the idea that perhaps, in the great scheme of things, one day their Lord Provider would remove humans from the world, or maybe it could be written in the human Book of Destiny that they be allowed to remain until, ultimately, they destroyed themselves with their own wickedness. He didn't know.

He didn't wish all of them ill, but he knew he would never be able to forgive those among them who had done such terrible things to his kind.

He pitied the others of them, who knew better, but were swept along on the same tide of ignorance, selfishness and greed, which, however long it took, he was sure would destroy them all in the end.

In the meantime, all he could do was to encourage the survivors of human cruelty who found their way to him, to take strength from their faith in their Lord Provider, and to carry on with their lives as best they could, for the sake of their little ones.

He was acutely conscious that badgers, in common with all the other creatures living in the wild, must keep an ever-watchful eye open to attempt to anticipate from where the next, of the myriad of threats people posed to their lives and homes, was coming. He knew the ills of the world wouldn't be cured in his lifetime.

Remembering that his own kind were not alone in their suffering, his mind would wander on then to other victims of mindless, senseless cruelty at the hands of Man.

Migrating birds regularly brought tales from faraway places where bulls were deliberately goaded and humiliated, before dying a horrible and painful death, merely for the entertainment of human spectators.

It was a sobering thought that even the very large and physically powerful were rendered helpless against the calculated cruelty of those humans who chose to indulge the dark side of human nature.

The bulls he had met at home seemed honest enough fellows, doing no harm to anyone, so why any humans would want to hurt them, or would want to see them being hurt, remained a complete mystery to him.

Cattle were protective of their families it was true, and, obviously with good reason, suspicious of humans, but they were amiable enough and most certainly deserved to be treated with understanding and respect.

He thought that those people who enjoyed the spectacle of an animal suffering torture and a violent death must themselves possess a very peculiar outlook on life.

He knew of no animal at all who would have the interest, let alone the desire, to do the same to a human.

Quite obviously, humans were not the intellectual superiors of all other life on Earth they fondly imagined themselves to be.

Epilogue

The day began much the same as any other.

The boys had their breakfast with Felix and then they went outside. It was a really beautiful day in late June and already the sunshine was warm.

They spent the early morning on the seashore, wandering along the wet sand, enjoying the sensation of it oozing up between their toes.

Then they watched the fishermen on the jetty for a while, who were busy lifting their catches of fish from their boats on to the quay. They felt sad for the fishes, who now lay dead in what was to them the alien environment of dry land.

From the end of the jetty, the two young cats had watched others of them so often darting about in the clear water, completely at one with their watery home.

"C'mon Mac," said Korky at last, "let's go back."

"Yes, let's." agreed Mac.

They made their way back to the gate, and then up the flights of steps on to the honeysuckle walk.

It was then that they saw the figure of Felix approaching.

"It's a bit early for his stroll," commented Korky to Mac, "I wonder what he's doing."

When he was near enough for them to speak to him, both thought Felix looked tired, and Korky said, "We're just on our way back, but shall we come back down with you?"

"No, no," said Felix hurriedly, "I won't be long, just a bit of a stroll ….. er, on my own."

"Are you sure you're all right?" asked Mac quietly.

"Yes, positive, but thank you for asking." Then he smiled at them both, passed them, and went on his way.

"I hope he's okay." said Korky.

"Yes, so do I." replied Mac.

Korky and Mac continued on their way. They stayed by the pond for a while, enjoying the sunshine as they watched the dragonflies and damsel flies hovering above its still waters, and it was not until Mac noticed that Felix was coming back along the honeysuckle walk, that they decided to carry on across the pond and up the hill to the barn. They didn't want Felix to think they were keeping an eye on him. He wouldn't have liked that.

They hurried on their way, unnoticed by Felix, and, by the time he arrived back in the yard, both boys were innocently sitting next to Fionn, who had just come out from the farmhouse.

The boys were concerned to notice that Felix seemed to be a bit breathless after his walk.

"Hello, you two." said Felix, smiling cheerily, and, turning to face Fionn, he said, "Good morning, old friend, you really should get up earlier you know, you've missed the best part of the day on a day like this."

"At my age, there's nothing I want to see, or do nowadays, which needs to be seen or done earlier in the day than this." said Fionn. He grinned at his friend, "You always were the early bird ….. I really don't know where you get your energy from."

Felix smiled and nodded, but said nothing. Just at the moment, he felt anything but energetic.

For the remainder of the morning, the three cats sat, chatting to Fionn.

By early afternoon, Fionn was asleep again, and Korky and Mac were happily sparring together in the sunshine.

Felix regarded his boys. They were laughing and joking as they bobbed and weaved before each other. He smiled to himself. His boys were boys no longer. They were fine, strong young adults, who, despite the trials and tribulations they had faced before they came to The Bothy, were now happy, well adjusted characters, who were fit and able to face whatever challenges might lay ahead of them in their lives.

He was satisfied that he and Fionn had done a good job both in raising Korky, and in restoring Mac's happiness and confidence. All the anxiety and hard work involved had been very well worthwhile and, when the time came – whenever that might be – for he and Fionn to leave them, they could do so without heavy hearts. Korky and Mac had formed a strong bond of friendship between them, and, whatever the future held for them, that friendship would see them through to the end of their days.

Felix turned to look at Fionn. He smiled fondly at his old friend, remembering the tiny blue-eyed puppy who had arrived at The Bothy all those long years ago.

Now Fionn was lying fast asleep, with his huge old head and neck draped down across his front legs and paws, the all grey muzzle twitching to the dictates of his adventures in a private world of dreams.

Felix sighed for all the happy days of their youth which were long gone now, and then smiled again as he thought of his own good fortune to have had such a wonderful family and friends around him over the years. He had surely been blessed.

And what a truly beautiful day it was today. He thought about it, and decided it was one not to be wasted. He would take another stroll on the seashore before teatime.

As Felix slipped away unnoticed by the others, none of the four friends was aware that destiny was about to call upon them again that afternoon, and Felix would never make it back to the yard, and his friends, after his walk.

This was to be the day on which Korky's prophesy would be fulfilled. Later in the day, Felix would be found lying peacefully in his favourite spot beside the pyramid rock, where he had fallen asleep on his way back from his walk on the seashore. But he was not there. He was already reunited with his beloved fiancée and his family beyond the end of the rainbow.

Unaware their benefactor was gone from them, the two boys played on, and, nearby, Felix's old friend, Fionn, slept on in the sunshine.

THE END

Korky

Courtesy of Prue Buck